Her Christmas Cowboy

Carsen Brothers Sweet Clean Western Romance, Volume 1

Marie Richards

Published by Marie Richards, 2021.

HER CHRISTMAS COWBOY

The Carsen Brothers of Sweet Rivers Ranch Book 1
(Sweet Clean Marriage of Convenience Western Romance)
By Marie Richards
Copyright 2021 Marie Richards

This book is a work of fiction. The names, characters, places, and incidents are products of the writer's imagination or have been used fictitiously. Any resemblance to persons, living or dead, is entirely coincidental.

ACKNOWLEDGEMENTS

Thank you, Lord, for all my blessings. To my amazing family and friends for your love and support. To my wonderful editors Allison and Jane.

This is a work of fiction. Similarities to real people, places, or events are entirely coincidental.

HER CHRISTMAS COWBOY

First edition. May 5, 2021.

Copyright © 2021 Marie Richards.

ISBN: 979-8201167790

Written by Marie Richards.

Table of Contents

Her Christmas Cowboy 1

Chapter 1 2

Chapter 2 13

Chapter 3 19

Chapter 4 26

Chapter 5 37

Chapter 6 49

Chapter 7 59

Chapter 8 66

Chapter 9 71

Chapter 10 76

Chapter 11 79

Chapter 12 84

Chapter 13 90

Chapter 14 93

Chapter 15 100

Chapter 16 103

Chapter 17 109

Chapter 18 113

Chapter 19 116

Chapter 20 119

Chapter 21 122

Chapter 22 124

Epilogue 126

Her Cowboy Hero 128

Chapter 1 129

Chapter 2 134

Her Christmas Cowboy

Luke Carsen needs to honor the stipulation in his late adoptive father's will for him to be married in order to take co-ownership of the family ranch. But he's too broken to love again. Recovering from the wounds of war is one thing, but the wounds from a previous relationship is another.

Jemma Smith grants wishes for the ill through her *Grant-A-Wish* app, but can she grant her dying grandfather's last wish to see her settle down before Christmas? She'd always dreamed of getting married and knows her grandfather just wants to see her happy, but she's not getting any younger and it's too late for her now, isn't it?

After meeting Luke through his matchmaking aunt, Sue Mae, Jemma wonders if she could make this work. Or will a marriage of convenience be all they can handle to appease their folks?

Chapter 1

"You can't be serious!" Luke Carsen said incredulously. He adjusted his cowboy hat while he stood in the Law Office of Charles & Son in Sweet Rivers, Texas, for the reading of Chet Carsen's will.

Chet Carsen was an eccentric philanthropist, a decorated war hero and Luke's adopted father. In fact, due to Chet's injuries during the Vietnam war, Chet couldn't have children of his own, so he and his wife, Alanna, adopted a dozen kids from the foster care system over the years. Six of them, including Luke's adopted brothers, Beau, Jesse, Chase, Jake, and Zack now grown men in their thirties, were all present now at the law firm, along with Sue Mae, their eighty-one-year-old eccentric aunt, Chet's twin sister, whose job was to make sure the boys all kept in line.

The brothers were not related by blood, but by bond, by loyalty, by their *adoptive* family, the Carsens. Each came from heartbreaking backgrounds that brought them to the foster care system and they were all eventually adopted by the great Chet Carsen when they were from the ages of ten to thirteen, an impressionable time in their lives. But their bond was as strong as blood. They looked out for each other. Family came first. Always.

They were blessed to find a good home and live on the ranch with miles and miles of green pastures, rolling hills, galloping horses, and grazing livestock. They had plenty of fresh air and wide-open spaces growing up on the ranch. But most of all, they had Chet and Alanna's love.

The fireplace in the office was framed with a beautiful Christmas garland, reminding Luke it was a month before Christmas. It had been a year since his dear old man passed.

"Is this some kind of joke?" his brother Beau added to the conversation.

"No sons, this is no joke," Joe Charles, the long-time family attorney said. "Your beloved adoptive father made it clear as day in his will. If you're to stay on the family ranch and take ownership...well, you need to be in a family. Married."

Joe sat with a serious expression on his face. He was dressed in a pristine suit with a shirt and tie along with his cowboy hat. He always wore his cowboy hat with this suit. He and Chet had been close over the last forty years. He was one of his father's closest friends.

"It's an all or nothing deal, boys." Joe looked each of Chet's adopted sons in the eyes.

"What's that supposed to mean?" Beau asked.

"It means Chet knew how much you all grew to care for each other. And he wanted you all to share that love with a spouse too. He knew you all had a lot to give. So you all must be married, not just one of you. So you better not let each other down."

Each of the cowboys exchanged glances with the others in the room.

"If you want the ranch to be transferred to your names to continue Chet's legacy..." the lawyer continued, "then you'll need to be hitched."

"This is not some sort of reality game show. This is our father's legacy we want to continue—can't believe we have to jump through hoops. You say we must get married before we can claim ownership in the ranch? We're not contestants vying for a prize."

"You're right about that. You're cowboys. You're Chet's boys. He loved you all and raised you to be good men. And you have so much to offer a wife and family of your own. He wants you to be happy, but you're all too stubborn to let go of the past. This is his way of giving you a little encouragement."

"You mean a little ultimatum," Luke said.

Luke loved his old man as if he were his biological father, and there wasn't anything he wouldn't do for Chet, but this? This was too much. Being wounded in Afghanistan was one thing. He could heal from that. But he didn't think he could heal from what his ex-wife did to him when he was away fighting for his country. He didn't want to go down that marriage road again.

The boys hadn't planned to follow in their adoptive father's footsteps serving in the military, but then the tragedy of 9/11 happened when they were barely adults. At the ages of seventeen through nineteen, they had had a sense of unity and patriotism like many Americans. It was a call to action. A record-breaking number of Americans enlisted in active duty or joined the enlisted reserves during the years following the attacks on 9/11.

The Carsen family was seated in the office after the reading of Chet Carsen's will, a decorated Vietnam War hero, who recently passed away at 80 years young. Chet Carsen, their beloved adoptive father was owner of the place they all now call home, *Chet Carsen's Sweet Rivers Family Ranch & Retreat.*

Chet worked most of his life on the ranch since he left the war. He even tried to beat the record of the oldest Texas cowboy to work on the ranch, a ninety-one-year-old who passed after climbing off his horse in the fields back in 1989—a rancher named Blasingame.

Chet was eighty when he stopped working in the fields. That was when six of his adopted sons all came back to Texas to help out on the ranch. He already had some help, but since he'd opened up part of the ranch as a retreat for the public, things hadn't been the same. It was the largest family-owned ranch in the district.

Many say that Chet died of a broken heart when his wife of fifty years, Alanna passed earlier last year. He'd died six months after her.

Luke and his adoptive brothers had moved off the ranch when they became adults, to either serve in the military or work in different businesses out of town. Sadly, they'd all experienced tragedy or heartbreak in their love lives by the time Chet started getting weak and needed them.

Luke, Beau and Jesse shared the same grief of having their significant other betray them, so they understood each other's pain. Beau was also a widow. His other adoptive brother, Jake, was happily married but then sadly lost his beloved wife and daughter in a tragic accident. Chase and Zack found it hard to connect with a soul mate.

They were only too happy to help in any way they could for the man who'd given them a second chance at a happy normal family upbringing. Maybe it was the Lord's way of bringing them together at the right time. Everything happens for a reason, Chet would always tell the boys. He also told them to always count their blessings, not their troubles, because there was always something to be thankful for.

Man, Luke missed his old man.

"It's not that bad, boys," Sue Mae said. Sue Mae was active in the women's ministry at the Sweet Rivers Church. She was also known to be a secret matchmaker for a lot of the couples in the church. Was she going to have a hand in making sure the men got married before the deadline?

Sue Mae was called the sewing queen because she always had a pair of needles in her hands, knitting something or sewing buttons for people and mending garments—like right now. She was busy knitting a cardigan. She said it helped calm her. It was relaxing.

Luke wished he could be relaxed right now.

Sue Mae was someone who joined garments together as well as people. She loved to matchmake on the side as if it were a hobby. She boasted once that she was responsible for half the couples getting together in her large Bible study class.

"Of course, it's that bad," Beau added. He'd vowed too, to never marry again. Beau's now late wife was killed in an accident—alongside her lover. The double tragedy of that day and the grief over losing her made him vow to never marry again or allow his heart to be crushed like that.

"Can't we just contest the will?" Luke paced by the fireplace in the office, his cowboy boots making a clunking sound on the hardwood floor.

"I'm afraid not, Luke," Joe said. "Now you know as much as I do that your father's will has the stipulation that if anyone contests the will, they get nothing."

Luke flinched. "You know as much as I do, it's not about the money. I don't care about any of that. I do care about being told how to run my life..."

And truth be told, the ranch *was* his life now.

He and five of his brothers had just moved back there after some time. Messy divorces, broken relationships. They'd each vowed to come back to their beloved family ranch where they grew up and carry on Chet's legacy and...remain single for the rest of their lives.

For what they'd all been through, they knew that family was more important—and they were determined not to let anybody else in—ever again.

After all, it hadn't worked out the first time around.

Besides, they weren't getting any younger. They'd concluded that marriage didn't work in modern times.

It wasn't like Chet's days. People changed. They weren't as committed as they were back in the old days. At least that's what Luke and his brothers told themselves to carry on without too much bruising to their egos.

Luke hadn't been to church on a regular basis much since that unfortunate incident with his ex-wife. He knew he should go back, but right now...

"I can't have Chet telling me how to live my life...from the grave," Luke added

"From beyond the grave?" his brother Chase added with a grin.

"It's not funny, Chase. I'm serious."

"Man, you're not the only one who's been affected. Can't believe Dad would pull a last joke like that on us."

Chet Carsen was not only a beloved decorated veteran and community activist who fought to help build up the community and help the disadvantaged, but he had secretly co-written sweet romances with his wife Alanna under the pen name C. C. Dale. No one knew it was them, except their close family members.

What Chet loved most was the ranch life, the stars at night, and love stories. It was love that helped Chet cope with the horrors of the war. That and the beautiful love letters he'd received from Alanna. His wife had given him some love stories along with some scriptures to read while he was away at war. He kept it close to his heart ever since. Chet believed that love could heal anything. Love made the world go round. And he believed that God made family so that family could show the strength of that love.

That's why he'd named the ranch *Sweet Rivers Family Ranch and Retreat*. The sign leading into the ranch read, "*From our family to yours.*" Plain and simple.

He wanted the family to continue there after he was gone. After all, the estate had a dozen or so beautifully-designed cozy log cabins that could each fit a family.

The main house and the main lodge housed a few guests who wanted a small retreat with their family.

How on earth could single folks run a family ranch? It just wasn't happening.

Chet had believed in love and family and he wanted that for his adopted sons. He knew they'd been broken up by disappointments in their love lives, but Chet also lost a love before meeting Alanna and he never gave up.

Chet always said the Lord had a way of working things out. He and his wife were able to foster kids who didn't have parents to take care of them. And that had turned out to be a blessing to all of them.

"You can't believe your old man would pull a joke like that on you?" the lawyer echoed, incredulously. "What makes you think it was a joke?" Joe asked, adjusting his glasses over his nose.

"Because Dad was always one to pull pranks like that," Zack, the youngest of the siblings at twenty-nine going-on-thirty, couldn't wait to chime in.

"He wants to be one of those famous authors who writes from the grave, only difference is he's trying to write our life stories too," Jake chimed in.

"You mean love stories," Beau added.

"Boys, you know how much this means to your dad. He's going to be honored soon with the local library being named after him in in two months. He didn't just write about romance, he believed in it. He believed in the magic of love and happiness and he knows you've all been hurt before. You know Chet was married before he met Alanna, but he doesn't want you to give up on finding love."

Joe then looked disdainfully at Jake's smart phone while he sent a text message to a client. "That's the trouble with you boys," he said. "You have more of a relationship with your gadgets than you do with women."

"Hey, now you know that's not fair," Jake said.

"Isn't it? You stare at your screen all day, do you even know what a real woman looks like in 3-D?"

Now it was Luke's turn to grin.

Luke then sighed. "Okay, let's get back on the discussion at hand now."

"The fact is, gentlemen, your father would like for you all to settle down and get married. And have children of your own. Have a loving family and life partner."

"Back in Chet's days it was a lot easier than it is today."

"How so?"

He shrugged.

"I'll tell you how. People didn't have all these distractions like they do now," Joe said, firmly.

"That's got nothing to do with it," Jake said.

"No?" Joe challenged.

"Anyway, I don't believe in love," Jake added.

"And why not?" Joe said, "Because people can barely find enough time to love themselves? They're too busy staring into their smartphones and their social media app waiting for people they don't ever see in person to like them."

Luke playfully rolled his eyes and shook his head. "So what do we need to do? I've got to be back at the ranch by noon."

"Well, I want you to seriously think about what I've said. It would make your father smile from above knowing that his sons were settled down by the time they reached thirty-five or forty. You have a year. I'll need to see each of your marriage certificates before the land ownership transfers to your names."

"A year?" Zack asked.

"Oh, really now?" Luke said softly. He loved his father more than anything in the world, but how could his old man make such a request in his will?

"How will we meet someone and get married in that time?" Zack added.

It wasn't reasonable.

Still, he would think about what he said, but he wasn't about to ruin his track record of keeping his heart safe from heartbreak.

He could remember what his now ex-wife did to him as if it was yesterday. It cut a hole in his heart, a hole too large to fill. It was worse than a bullet wound because this was from someone he'd trusted, someone he'd loved, someone he'd given his heart and soul to.

It started off with a text message.

Missing you, Trav.

Can't wait to see you again.

Can't believe I'm having your baby.

I just hope my husband doesn't find out it's not his. Hope it looks like me.

A sick feeling rushed into his stomach just thinking about that horrible text. His blood ran cold, his heart stopped pumping that very minute. The minute his world came crashing down over him.

He was stunned. Shocked. Humiliated. Angry. Words could not fully capture his broken heart. He really loved Maxine. He could not believe she did this. And on top of that he got the message. Not this Travis fella.

"Maybe, the good Lord wanted you to get that message," Sue Mae had said to Luke when he told her that day, "so that you could see what was going on behind your back."

"You really think so?" Luke had asked her, with disbelief.

"Yes, I do. That's what happens when you put your trust in the Lord and you do the right thing, and you ask him for guidance and protection. He reveals things to you. Now let me make you some sweet tea and we'll read a scripture."

That was another thing about his aunt Sue Mae, who never liked to be called aunt, just Sue Mae. She believed that "sweet tea and a scripture" could solve anything.

He smiled at that memory and that sentiment. He and his brothers were glad to have Sue Mae around, living on the ranch with them at the main house, now that his adoptive parents were no longer with them.

Right now, he didn't know if he wanted that revelation, though deep down he knew it was for the best.

Luke had been bitter about the whole idea about love and marriage ever since. Of course, he ended up divorcing Maxine. And now Maxine was with Travis and their child.

But Luke would never recover from that. Ever. He could never trust a woman again. He knew the Bible always said to forgive, but he was having a hard time forgetting right now. Torn and confused about what happened. While he was serving in the military, his wife was back home serving another man.

How could he ever believe in love again?

Never again.

He could never trust again. Anyone. So what if he buried himself in his work? It was safer that way.

Then when he got news from Texas that his adoptive father wasn't doing too well, he moved back home to help out at the ranch.

Trust was something that would take him years to repair. How could he ever trust a woman again? There was no way he could ever marry.

Chapter 2

"I'm really sorry, Jemma." Dr. Samuels held the clipboard to his chest while Jemma Smith sat in his office. "There's nothing more we can do."

A wave of nausea crashed over her. She tried to grab onto something to steady herself.

"Are you okay, Jemma?" the doctor asked, concerned.

"Yes, I just can't believe…Are you sure about this, doc?" she asked, in disbelief.

"Yes, Jemma. Your grandfather is not doing too well. There's no easy way to say this but…he may not make it to Christmas."

Her heart squeezed in her chest. She could not breathe. Her lungs burned.

It was a month before Christmas.

She could lose her beloved grandfather in a month?

She shook her head in disbelief, unable to process the doctor's words.

"No." Her whispered shock was mostly to herself.

"I'm sorry again, Jemma."

Doc Samuels glanced at his watch. She knew he had rounds to make at the hospital.

"Thanks, doc."

"Listen, if there's anything I can do. Please let me know."

She swallowed hard. "Just pray for grandpa, doc. The more prayers, the better."

Her words were soft, her throat felt as if it was closing in. She was in shock.

Her grandfather was her only family left. He'd raised her after her parents were killed by a drunk driver when she was young. It had been a devastating blow to the family—a horrific tragedy.

If it hadn't been for her grandfather, she didn't know what she'd have done or what her life would have become. He'd taken care of her and given her so much in her life.

He helped put her through college and was always there as a support, a guide. And now? He needed her.

"By the way," the doctor said before leaving. "This is for you." He handed her a card.

"What's this?" She opened it.

"It's a thank you note from the staff here. What you did for little Jimmy was...it was very thoughtful and kind, Jemma. You made his day."

Jemma's heart sank when she thought of little Jimmy with cerebral palsy.

"It was nothing, really. He's going through so much—it's the least we can do."

By we, she meant, her.

She'd started her wish-making service for deserving patients while she was in college. It was mostly online and through an app.

It was called *Jemma's Grant-A-Wish* app that connected critically ill children or adults and their caregivers with organizations that could grant their life-changing wishes. Sort of like a matchmaking app for wishes. It was a non-profit app that had been so close to her heart.

It was in its early stage, but she hoped it would grow and develop into something bigger and could reach out to many beyond Sweet Rivers and the state of Texas.

She ran it out of her home that she shared with her grandfather. It was more of a heart project. She'd spent most of her time taking care of her grandfather and working online freelancing for clients. But she also worked on her *Grant-A-Wish* app, pairing ill children, ill adults, and injured war vets with organizations that could make their dreams come true. She would, of course, vet each organization carefully. Her foundation was doing fairly well, and she hoped to bring it wider in the future.

"*Jemma's Grant-A-Wish* app is amazing! You've made so many wishes come true for the sick and dying."

The irony of it all was that she was the founder of *Jemma's Grant-A-Wish*.

She could help others make their wishes come true. But who was going to help her make her wish of having more time with her dear grandfather come true?

That was probably too tall an order to ask for, wasn't it?

Moments later, Jemma found herself at her grandfather's bedside. She'd just finished helping him with his meal.

"Jemma, darling, you look sad."

"Sorry, Grandpa. I'm supposed to be cheering you up."

"It's no trouble, darling. I'm not afraid, don't worry."

Her heart squeezed in her chest.

"Grandpa, I…"

"Jemma, I'm so proud of you. I just want you to know that."

"I know, Grandpa. And I'm so proud of you too."

"I want you to be happy."

"I *am* happy. Well, I would be happier if you were home right now, but..."

"It's all right, Jems. When I say I want you to be happy, you know what I mean."

"Oh, no. Not that again," she said, lovingly with a smile of appreciation, trying to lighten the mood. "We're not going down that road again."

"Jemma, you're a lovely young woman. You work so hard. You always want to make people happy. I know you'll find a nice man to marry. I know it's what you've always wanted."

He was right.

Jemma had dreamed of being a bride her whole life. Dreamt of marrying Mr. Right and starting a family before it was too late. She'd even dress up in white and wear a pretend veil over her head. Her grandfather used to lovingly tease her about it.

When she was a child, she'd play with her dolls and pretend the male and female dolls were a happily married couple—just like her parents had been.

It had been her dream to one day get married and start a family of her own.

But then her ex had crushed that dream.

She'd cried for a week and wouldn't come out of her room after his betrayal. She'd almost given up on finding true love.

Her grandfather had been there to console her. He was always her rock. That's why she threw herself in her business and kept helping others to fill that void in her life while feeling good about giving back and making others happy.

But her grandfather knew in her heart, she wished things had worked out between her ex and her.

She wanted to have what her parents had. They were so in love and so happy as a family—before that horrible day.

Now, she was in her early thirties.

He just didn't want her to give up on that dream.

And he didn't want her to miss out on marital bliss.

He also desperately wanted to know that she would not be alone when he left this place and that she'd carry on his family line.

That meant a lot to him. And she knew it.

But her heart was beyond repair now.

The damage was irreversible as far as she was concerned. She didn't want to get hurt again. She couldn't withstand that kind of heartbreak again. She'd vowed not to put her heart on the line again like that. She had to remember that.

"Grandpa, we've already been through this. I don't think it's meant to be."

And she meant it.

She was engaged once, to Thomas. But he'd broken her heart, crushed it to a million pieces when he left her for her best friend, her college roommate.

The thought caused her skin to prickle with heat.

There was no way she would ever trust a man again or go through that again. It just wasn't worth the pain. She started to doubt herself after that.

Was she a little too thick in the thighs? Too shy? Not adventurous enough?

Her roommate had been the fun one. While Jemma was the shy, bookworm who loved to figure out ways to make the world a better place. She always felt a sense of awkwardness in crowds or social settings.

It took her a while to dig herself out of that mental hole. She still could not believe Thomas had gone out with her college roommate behind her back. Her glamorous college roommate.

Unlike Jemma who'd always been the nice girl. The girl next door. The plain-Jane with big thighs.

No, Jemma wasn't built like a model like her roommate, whom she'd admired—up until the time she found out about her rendezvous with Thomas that is— but Jemma was all-heart and that had to count for something.

When it all went down, she'd thought something was wrong with her. She soon realized there was nothing wrong with her, only her choices could have been better.

"I wish I could live to see you settle down and get married. To see you happy, Jemma. You always said you wanted to get married."

Her grandfather's eyes filled up with tears. "That would be the most blessed Christmas gift I could have, to see you have the life you always dreamed of," Grandpa continued.

The heartache crushed her.

How could this be?

His final wish was to see her get married...before Christmas.

There was no way she could grant him that wish.

Where on earth would she even find a good man before then?

Jemma's *Grant-A-Wish* app granted wishes to the frail or dying. Could she even grant her own grandfather his last wish to see her get married by Christmas?

Chapter 3

"Now look, Luke, it's not as bad as you think?" Sue Mae said later at the main house after they'd gotten back to the ranch from the lawyer's office.

Sue Mae had already poured glasses of her famous Southern sweet tea, because what else did a person need in times of trouble. That and a scripture.

The scent of cornbread and pecan pie wafted from the oven. Sue Mae wasted no time in making her favorite dishes in the kitchen when she got back. She loved knitting, baking, making her famous sweet tea and reading a scripture. And she always invited the boys over and made sure her adoptive nephews were taken care of.

Though they each could cook a mean dish for themselves, they all liked to take turns, especially when in their own cabins.

"You know the Bible says He will give you beauty for your ashes. You need to know that everything will work out fine. This stipulation in the will is a blessing in disguise."

"What if it ends up being a curse?" Zack asked as he picked up his glass of sweet tea.

"It won't." Sue Mae had her hands on her hips and pursed her lips.

Sister Ellie was also there and baking her famous gingerbread cookies in the double oven in the kitchen. There was always more than one dish baking or cooking at the same time in that kitchen—just as it was when Alanna and Chet were around. The scent of ginger wafted in the air.

They'd already started decorating for Christmas.

It looked as if Sue Mae would be busy trying to convince the boys to settle down fast to fulfil their father's last wishes so they could also stay on the ranch.

"Sue Mae, I loved Chet more than anything in this world, God rest his soul," Luke said, "I'd do anything for him. That's why I moved back here to Texas to help him run the ranch when he got too tired, but there's just no way I'm getting married. I'm sorry, but I just can't."

"You say married like it's a bad thing, Luke," Sister Ellie chimed in.

"Marriage is a great institution," Sue Mae added. "You need to give it a try, or in many of your cases, give it another try. I don't understand you boys. You're such fine young men. Why can't you just make the effort to try again?"

"She's right," Sister Ellie said.

"Chet meant well," Luke said, "But marriage is not for everyone. Besides, we're not exactly in relationships right now. Our relationship is with the ranch and making sure our guests at the retreat are taken care of."

"That's right," Jesse said, grabbing a sandwich from the fridge. The man had a hearty appetite. He was always snacking on something. But then he worked it off on the ranch and at the gym facilities near the retreat section.

"Unless you count Jesse who has a relationship with the fridge," Beau added.

Beau was always the comedian in the group.

If Luke was being honest with himself, he'd sort of moved back to the ranch to avoid another marriage or thinking about relationships. Helping his father out had been his priority, of course, but he thought he could just focus on the land, taking care of the livestock and the occasional visitor to the retreat part of the ranch. His father had, in his later years, opened up the old lodge to families who wanted to spend a little time on a working ranch, catching the fresh air, closeness to nature, and time with the animals. They had a little horse-riding trail on the west side of the ranch. They often had visitors spend time there.

What he missed about his adoptive father was spending quality time on the ranch together, working with the animals, then spending time in the early evening watching the sunset and the animals grazing. That's what he missed. He missed the closeness. The quiet. The relaxation. The last thing he'd want was for a woman to come and stir his mind all up again, like his ex-wife had done.

She really messed him up.

The horses were loyal friends. His adoptive brothers were loyal.

He could handle that. Family always came first. But to Luke, that did not include love or falling in love again.

His heart was off the table.

Period.

He would just have to find some other way around that stipulation in his father's will.

Sue Mae laid out the gingerbread cookies on the tabletop, after Sister Ellie left the kitchen. They always worked together as a team in the kitchen. She then took off her apron and put it aside. The boys knew she was about to say something now. And they'd better listen up. That was their cue.

"Now boys, I know what you're all thinking. But you know how much this ranch meant to Chet."

"I know, Sue Mae," Luke's voice was soft and gentle. "And trust me, it means a lot to us too. That's why we all came back. This is our blood, our home, our heart."

"What you need to do is make room in your heart for a good wife."

Luke sighed deeply. His aunt was right. Deep down he knew it. But he wasn't about to give his heart to a woman again.

Beau held up his hand. "Uh, Sue Mae, just one thing."

"Yes, Beau." An amused grin perched on her lips.

"We don't exactly have anyone in our lives right now."

"Yeah, and the condition in the will, according to the lawyer is that we all have to be married in a year's time, tops! And since we're all in our thirties..." Luke took a sip of his sweet tea and the smooth refreshing taste sated his taste buds.

All this talk about marriage and wills made his throat as dry as the Sahara Desert.

"Yes, darling. I've thought of that." A sly grin curved Sue Mae's lips.

"You have?"

"Yes." Sue Mae's tone was warm and firm. "I'm going to arrange for you all to be married."

Luke almost choked on his sweet tea. He coughed a bit. "What?"

"What did you say?" Beau added.

The other brothers looked as stunned as Luke felt.

"An arranged marriage, darling. You need to fulfil that condition of the will or we won't have the family ranch anymore."

"Oh, no. Wait a minute." Luke cleared his throat. He could not believe what he was hearing. Sue Mae couldn't possibly be suggesting what he thought she was suggesting.

"Darling..."

"Are you talking about some sort of marriage of convenience?" Luke asked, incredulously.

"Yes. What's wrong with that?"

"Everything, Sue Mae. Is that even legal?"

"Well, of course it is, dear. How do you think your dear father and Alanna ended up together?"

"What? But...but I don't get it."

"What's there to get, sweetie. Some marriages start off as convenient and end up as a marriage of love."

"Yeah, and some marriages start off with love and end up as a marriage of convenience," Jesse added.

"What's that supposed to mean?" Luke asked Jesse.

"Oh, come on," Jesse replied. "Darla and I knew it was over. We only stayed because of, well, her father was the preacher of the church and it wouldn't look right if we got divorce. But we never even spoke to each other most of the time. She was always out travelling all over the world with her business. It's like we were just together in name only. Then, of course, later, she ran off with some aristocrat in Europe."

Luke's heart ached for his brother. He knew how much Chase loved Darla. But she didn't feel the same way and then she ended up leaving him anyway—for another man.

He thought of the irony that he and two of his brothers all had unfaithful spouses. That's why it would take a whole lot of *faith* for them to believe in love again.

How would they find someone who understood where they were coming from?

But Sue Mae's revelation that his adoptive parents were a marriage of convenience really knocked him sideways.

"So Chet and Alanna were set up?"

"Well, yes. You see, your father had just come back from the war and his first wife had died soon after. It was tragic in so many ways. After his injuries from the war, he couldn't have kids. He wanted a wife and family so badly though. He ended up going through an arrangement with someone looking for a husband. And well, it worked out. They agreed to make it work and they did. And they later adopted children, all of you, as their family when they were nearing middle-age. Now, you see. Marriages of conveniences *can* work out."

Luke thought about that for a moment. He may agree to this marriage of convenience thing for the sake of keeping the ranch. Fine. But he was never going to fall in love again. And that's that. But he and his brothers still had another obstacle.

"So how are we to find these mail order brides then?" Luke asked, in disbelief at the whole situation. When he'd gone to the reading of the will this morning, he had no idea his life would be turned upside down with this stipulation.

Beau chuckled. "I don't think they do mail order brides these days, do they?"

"You'd be surprised," Sue Mae said at the table. She arched her brow with a sly grin on her lips.

If Luke didn't know any better, he'd swear Sue Mae and her cousin Sister Ellie were cooking something up, other than whatever it was in the oven.

"Sue Mae will handle all the matchmaking here," Sister Ellie said, walking back into the kitchen. "She'll get you settled with the right brides."

"What? Sue Mae?" Luke asked, incredulously.

"Yes, of course," Sue Mae said. "I'm a good judge of character. And...in this town, I know everybody."

"You mean you know everybody's *business*," Sister Ellie chimed in with a wicked grin.

"Excuse me." Sue Mae feigned being insulted.

Sister Ellie grinned. "On a more serious note, we need to get going on this thing so that we can give Joe the update at the law firm. He needs to turn over the ranch in the boys' names but not until they've fulfilled Chet's last wish on the will. That's the deal."

Luke rubbed his forehead. He couldn't believe he was even thinking about going through with this. Having his dear old aunt Sue Mae set him up with a bride.

Could this really happen?

Chapter 4

"You are amazing, Jemma," Mrs. Tendril said. "You arranged for Jimmy to visit a ranch and ride a horse?" Jimmy's mother looked so pleased.

They sat in the living room of Jimmy's home on the east side. It was a modest apartment filled with toys and medical accessories for Jimmy to help him with his condition. They had a small Christmas tree in the corner of the living room with a few lovely decorations on it.

Seemed like most people began their festivities earlier when they had little children around. Jemma hadn't had time to put decorations up, especially since she'd been spending more time at the long-term care wing of the hospital with her grandfather.

Mrs. Tendril, Jimmy's mom, had a pleasant smile on her face, yet she looked worn out. Like a devoted mother who didn't get much sleep.

Jemma was so glad she was able to help her get some respite while a nurse and she took Jimmy to the ranch.

Jemma could feel the excitement bursting through the woman. She was so glad she was able to grant little Jimmy his wish through her *Grant-A-Wish* app.

She knew about the Sweet Rivers Family Ranch and Retreat owned by the late Chet Carsen. She'd visited there a few times already but never had the chance to meet the brothers.

In fact, her grandfather used to be friends with Chet. They'd served together on the same unit during the war.

"Hey, it's no trouble at all."

"No really, it's wonderful. We really appreciate it."

"It's the least we could do. So I spoke to someone at the ranch and they said the ranch foreman would be happy to make that happen. The foreman's name is Luke Carsen, he's one of the adopted sons of Chet Carsen."

"You know the Carsens personally?"

The Carsens were huge in Sweet Rivers, Texas. Almost everybody knew them or knew *of them.*

They had a solid reputation and a whole lot of heart. She admired the way the family ran the ranch and opened up its doors to the needy and those who were suffering. She'd respected the brothers' work on the ranch but never got up close to them.

"Well, sort of. My grandfather and Chet Carsen used to be good friends."

"Oh, nice. And by the way, how is your grandfather doing?"

Jemma swallowed hard.

Her heart still ached thinking about him, his last wish, and how she could grant anybody their wishes except her own grandfather. Especially now that he only had possibly weeks left.

Oh, the thought tore away at her. That's why she wanted to spend every waking second with him, but he wouldn't let her. He told her that she didn't need to stay at the hospital with him twenty-four seven. He was probably just preparing her for when the time finally came.

She tried to brush that awful thought away from her mind for the moment.

He'd told her so many times, tearfully, how he wished he could have seen her get settled down and married before he went to be with the Lord.

There was no way she'd be able to marry by Christmas to give his soul some peace. If only she could, but it was no use. She wasn't even dating anybody right now.

And she'd planned it that way a long time ago after Thomas. There was no way she was setting her heart on the line like that again. No way.

"He's fine," Jemma said softly, trying to avert the woman's gaze. She didn't want to get into the prognosis. She was there for her clients. Her private life was not something she was going to trouble them with. She wouldn't want to burden anybody with her personal problems.

"Good," Mrs. Tendril said. "I'm glad to hear it."

"Well, Jimmy's going to have a wonderful time at the ranch." Jemma changed the subject back to the ranch trip to lighten her mood.

Her heart ached every time she thought about her grandfather. She just wanted to spend as much time with him, knowing now that he didn't have much time left.

But more than anything, she deeply regretted not being able to make his last wish come true.

"So you asked the ranch foreman about Jimmy going there tomorrow and he said it would be okay?"

"Well, actually, I spoke with his aunt, Sue Mae."

She was so glad that Sue Mae had encouraged her to use Sweet Rivers Family Ranch and Retreat.

In fact, Sue Mae had been such a wonderful ear to her struggles when she needed someone to talk to. Sue Mae knew about the struggles she was having with her grandfather's health and all that was going on in her life and how saddened and disappointed her grandfather was in her that he wouldn't live to see her married. Sue Mae had been nothing but encouraging.

"You asked his aunt?"

"Yes. She helps run the ranch. She's Chet Carsen's sister," Jemma continued. "She's also coordinator of the church youth drama club and active in the women's ministry. I've known her since then...when I was much younger, of course. It's a wonderful family ranch. Six of Chet's twelve adopted sons also live on the ranch and help run it. That's quite a dynamic team there. They'd be so happy to have you visit and stay at their lodge."

"Sounds wonderful."

"So we can meet tomorrow at ten o'clock in the morning, if that's okay with you."

"Ten o'clock sounds great."

"Good. Ten o'clock it is then," Jemma felt a warm satisfaction that she was finally closer to helping little Jimmy's wish come true.

***

Later that morning, Jemma met up with her friend Mandy at Sweet Rivers Café.

Jemma hugged the cup of hot cocoa with marshmallows. That used to comfort her when she was younger. Hot cocoa on a crisp wintery day.

"You're not yourself," Mandy commented.

"I guess you could say that."

Mandy was always the cheerful, perceptive friend. She had naturally curly red hair and freckles on her face. It didn't seem to bother her when she was teased about it back in college. Jemma always thought her hair and freckles looked lovely and gave her a nice southern charm. That's probably why they'd bonded back then. Jemma was the heavier, curvy girl with the thick thighs and Mandy was the girl with the freckles.

"What's wrong, girl? For someone who's known for making other people's wishes come true, I sure wish I could make you smile."

"Mandy, you're a true friend. I just...there's a lot on my mind, right now."

"Like what? Are you going to keep me guessing or what?" Mandy smiled warmly.

Mandy never liked to see anyone upset. That's probably why she ended up going into social work.

Jemma took some social work courses in college too, as electives, but then she branched out into sociology and business. She wanted to do something that made a difference in this world. Set up an organization that helped others. After losing her parents in that crash when she was much younger, she was devastated, and she'd always wished it never happened.

She wished someone could have reversed time and kept them safe. That never happened, of course, but a part of her longed to make others wishes come true.

She felt good when she could grant last wishes to the dying or wishes for ill children or war vets. To put a smile on their faces. That's what made it all worth it.

Of course, her grandfather stepped in and took custody of her after that fateful night, and she was so blessed to have him in her life.

He meant the world to her. He cared for her, made sure all her needs were met, he'd read to her at nights when she was much younger, and took her to church on Sundays and taught her how to pray.

There was nothing she wouldn't do for her grandpa. But he knew Jemma always dreamed of being happily married like her parents. And it broke his heart that he wouldn't live to see her fulfill her childhood dream.

She couldn't even grant him his last wish.

Besides, she was convinced there just weren't many good men left. All the good ones were spoken for, weren't they?

"It's my grandfather. He...he's not doing too well."

"Oh, no, girl. I'm so sorry to hear that. What's wrong with him?"

"Well, the doc said he doesn't have much time. The big C made a comeback and well, it could be before Christmas. He's not as strong as he used to be. I wish I could do something."

"Oh, Jemma, I'm so sorry he's not doing well. I'm sorry for what you're going through."

Jemma looked out the window of the café. She then turned her attention back to her friend.

"It's not just that, Mandy."

Mandy's eyebrows creased with concern.

"I'm afraid I just can't grant my grandfather his...his wish."

She didn't want to say his last wish or his dying wish.

Jemma knew he didn't have much time, but it was hard to face that right now, and speaking it out in the open would make it more true.

Right now, the truth was too much to bear. That's what she did sometimes, she tried to focus on the positives or not dwell too hard on the harsher side of life.

She knew she'd have to face it soon. But right now, she just wanted to believe in miracles. She wanted to believe that somehow she'd have more time with him than the doc had suggested.

"What do you mean you can't grant his wish? Did he ask you for something?" Mandy's voice was gentle. It almost made Jemma cry.

No wonder Mandy went into social work as a career. She was good at reaching out to people. Connecting with them. Making them feel as if they want to open up to her.

"Well, you remember my ex..."

Mandy frowned and shook her head. "Oh, yeah. I remember him all right. He didn't deserve you. That guy was a piece of work."

"I know."

"Listen, just be glad he left you when he did. Better earlier than later. You deserve so much better, Jemma. You're all heart and soul."

"Thanks, Mandy. Trouble is, Grandpa thinks so too."

"I don't get it. What's wrong with that?"

"Well, he's desperate to see me fulfill my childhood dream of being happily married like my parents. He knows I've always dreamed of that. Sharing my life with an amazing, loving life partner. He doesn't want to see me alone."

"Well, he's right, Jemma. You deserve so much better."

"Thanks, but you know I'm taking a very long break from the dating arena. My only love right now, besides Grandpa of course, is my work. My *Grant-A-Wish* app. Granting people the wishes of their heart. My work would never let me down, cheat on me or leave me. I feel happy when I can make others happy. Especially those who are down on their luck or dealing with a sickness or worse."

"I know, girl. I hear you. And you're doing so well with your foundation, but it doesn't mean you can't meet someone else."

"I know, but I thought my ex was the real deal." Jemma sighed deeply. "It breaks my heart that my grandfather won't get to see me happily married. That's his wish because he knows that's what I've always wanted." Jemma choked on her words, her heart filled with emotion.

"Oh, Jemma. You'll meet someone who appreciates you."

"Thanks, but where would I find a husband by Christmas?"

"Excuse me? By Christmas? You planning on wrapping him up and putting him underneath your grandpa's Christmas tree?"

Jemma grinned in spite of the seriousness of the situation. "No, silly. The doc said he may not have until Christmas. My grandpa. So, I would love to tell him that...well, if only I could get a fake guy..."

"A fake guy?"

"You know what I mean. A fake marriage. Only Grandpa wouldn't know it's fake. Just so that he could see that I've got what I always wanted. He'd be so happy."

"I see what you mean." Mandy lifted her cup of hot cocoa to her lips and thought for a moment.

"Hey maybe you can get a fake guy."

Now it was Jemma's turn to look confused.

"A fake guy?"

"Yeah, you know. Pay someone to..."

"Hey wait a minute. No way. I'm not doing that. You know what? The whole thing is a bad idea. It's not gonna happen. Grandpa would see right through it and not to mention the town. You know it's a small town, right? People talk."

"Oh, yeah. Tell me about it."

"Besides, I've got to think about the house we're leasing."

"You don't own it?"

"No, we had to sell our other house to help pay for Grandpa's medical expenses. Anyway, the house we lease now will be up for renewal soon."

"What are you going to do?"

"I don't know. I guess, I never thought that far. I used the last of my savings to help pay for Grandpa's medical equipment and scraped by with whatever freelance assignments I could do online to help pay my share of the rent. Grandpa's pension helped pay the other half. But..."

"Oh, no..."

Jemma swallowed hard. "Yes, when he...goes to be with the Lord, I'll be going to the women's shelter. There's no way I could afford rent on my little pay. That's the trouble. I have this great venture helping to grant wishes but it's not exactly a liveable source of income. I've been doing out of the goodness of my heart, not thinking ahead. My time has just been spent looking after Grandpa full time and working freelance gigs."

"Oh, Jemma. I...I don't know what to say. You know you could always stay with me."

"Thanks, Mandy. But I'm not putting you out like that. Besides, what would your roommate think?"

"Oh, don't worry about that."

"You know Grandpa used to say sometimes we can only do our best then we have to leave it in the hands of the Lord."

"True."

Right now, Jemma knew she needed a miracle. She didn't know how she was going to make ends meet or make it happen.

She didn't want to give up her app anytime soon, but it was time she started thinking about the future and a way to make a sustainable living. Maybe she could apply for some jobs online. Or maybe she should just try to get more business for her freelance writing gigs. She was good at writing blog posts for events. But would that be enough to cover her expenses?

Jemma sighed. "Listen, I've got to get everything ready for my gig tomorrow."

"Gig?"

"Yes, I'm bringing little Jimmy to the Sweet Rivers Family Ranch tomorrow."

"Aww, that is so sweet. He's gonna love it there."

"I hope so. He really wanted to ride one of the horses there."

"You know, there's a lot of cute cowboys on the Sweet Rivers Ranch."

"Mandy!"

"What? It's true. You know those Carsen boys are pretty hot. Everyone's talking about them. Heard they're all single too."

"Not gonna happen. Besides, I heard they're just not reachable."

"Reachable?"

"You know? Date wise. For some reason, their ranch is their life. Heard they don't have time for women—well, not anymore. They're either divorced or widowed or something like that. It's really weird. You would think they'd settle down and fill those cabins with families. I guess some people are just dedicated to their work and nothing else. Besides, maybe if they were all married, they'd have less time to make the Ranch retreat what it is. Who knows."

"Oh come on now. You don't really believe that do you?"

Jemma glanced at the time on her phone. "What I believe doesn't really matter here. What *they* do does. Anyway, I'm sure they have their reasons for staying single."

Chapter 5

Luke loved getting up at five o'clock in the morning before sunrise. It was a quiet time of the morning before the animals got up. He went to get everything set up to feed the cows.

His adoptive dad and he used to get up early together back in the day when he was much younger. Chet used to talk about getting energy for the day when you rise before the sunrise. They used to spend time talking a lot while working together. Oh, he missed those heart-to-heart moments. The memories came flooding back to him.

He missed Chet like crazy. Still, he was glad he kept some of those traditions going. Life on the ranch was a world away from working in the big city. He was glad it worked out that he had to come back to help his ailing father out with the ranch.

After serving his time in the military, he'd done a few stints in the corporate world. But not for long.

Instead of spending time in traffic, heading to the office, dealing with office politics, late nights in the boardrooms, making deals, and tracking sales, he'd be mending fences, tending to the land, and taking care of the precious livestock by feeding the cows by 6 a.m., filling up the water for the cows, feeding the chicken in the hen house, and making truck stops in town to the local feed and ranch supply store. And best of all, making sure their guests at the lodge retreat were taken care of.

He enjoyed taking the time in the morning to catch the breeze and to think.

And thinking of that, he could not believe what he'd heard yesterday in the lawyer's office. Was his father really serious about this?

But then again, he supposed the old man had no choice. It was, after all, supposed to be a family ranch. It even said so in the name.

He glanced up at the sign: *Welcome to Chet Carsen's Sweet Rivers Family Ranch & Retreat. From our family to yours.*

Our family.

Would he ever have a family of his own? He'd been down that country road before and he was not even thinking about travelling down that road again. It hurt too much when it didn't work out.

He got ready to feed the cows. He loved feeding the cows. Right now, they looked hungry. He gently patted one and then got everything set up and ready.

He had to remember his ten o'clock appointment with the *Grant-A-Wish* client. He'd be finished up here in no time and then have a shower before getting ready for the tour.

***

A few hours later, Sue Mae stopped by the horse stalls. "So glad you're able to take time out of your busy schedule to do this, Luke," she said, patting Randy, one of their horses.

"Hey, it's no trouble. You know how much I love kids." He just wished he could have one of his own one day.

But that was off the table since the child his now ex-wife was raising wasn't his to begin with. He wanted so badly to be a father and to show his kids the ropes, not just on the ranch but in life in general. So spending time helping out needy kids filled that part of his heart.

"Well, they'll be here soon."

"Good."

"I'm so glad you could take the boy out to pet Randy and maybe he can take a little ride. Depending on his condition."

"Of course."

Moments later, a young woman approached them.

Luke's gaze travelled to the young woman's pretty face. She was stunning. She wore nice hip-hugging jeans that accentuated her curves. A pink and white shirt that highlighted the blush in her cheeks. And her silky, long ebony hair cascaded down her shoulders. There was something about her that captured Luke's attention. It was her aura. She was gorgeous. And she had lovely large brown eyes framed by long lashes. Wow. He'd never seen such a well-put together beauty like that before.

She looked around as Luke came out of the stable with Randy.

"Oh, hi there," she said, waving. Her smile was as bright as her pretty eyes.

"Howdy." He tipped his cowboy hat.

"Jemma, you're right on time." Sue Mae beamed. She walked over to Jemma and held her arm while they walked toward Luke.

"Luke, this is Jemma Smith from *Jemma's Grant-A-Wish Foundation*. Jemma, this is Luke."

Luke was almost lost for words. "Nice to meet you."

He almost never got this nervous around a woman before.

"You two haven't actually met before, have you?" Sue Mae lit up when she spoke. "Luke, you remember Smith, your father's friend from the west."

"Oh, right."

"Well, this is his granddaughter." A wicked grin curved Sue Mae's lips, like she was up to something.

Then Luke saw Jemma's cheeks flush.

"Yes, I've been here a few times when I was younger. I think I saw you working on the ranch once," Jemma said, her voice smooth and sweet like honey.

"Oh, right. That was before I left."

"Before you left?"

"Yes, my brothers and I ended up pursuing other interests before coming back here to help out on the ranch."

"Luke and his brothers also served in the military," Sue Mae added with pride.

"That was very noble of you all," she said, her voice filled with emotion. "And I'm so sorry about your loss. Chet was a remarkable person. Always giving you a warm smile and words of wisdom. He had the gift to make everyone feel like family."

"Thanks," Luke said.

Her words sank right into Luke's soul. He didn't know what it was. It was something about the way she said it. It was her soft genuine tone, her warmth. There was something about her...

Stop that, Luke. It's no use. You're not going down that road again, remember? She's a lady. And you're supposed to be taking a break from them. A good long break.

Still, he couldn't help but gaze at Jemma's soft fingers. And man, did her hands look soft, yet strong. And those lips of hers. So shapely. He wondered if they were as soft as they looked.

No wedding band on her ring finger, not even a sign of a wedding band or engagement ring. He was just checking. Not that it would make a difference, because he was never dating again. But maybe, she'd be good for one of his brothers.

"It's been a year now." Luke fought to take control of the conversation and shift his focus back to the present. "Time flies. Still miss him around here."

Jemma seemed genuinely crushed by Chet's passing. He couldn't help but notice sadness filled her pretty brown eyes when he mentioned Chet's name.

And man, she was pretty. He'd met many women before, but she was different. There was just something sweet and precious about her aura. Her warm smile. And those lips. Man, she had the most shapely perfect lips he'd ever seen on a woman.

Sue Mae must have noticed his gaze on Jemma because she smirked. And he was sure that wasn't his imagination.

What was Sue Mae up to?

"So where is the little fella then?" Luke asked Jemma.

"Oh, he's at the cabin. I think he's in cabin number eight with his nurse. They'll be here soon," Jemma said. "Look, I really appreciate what you're doing. You have no idea. This means the world to little Jimmy. He's always wanted to come out here on a ranch and pet the horses. He loves animals."

"Hey, it's no trouble. Glad we can help."

Luke's heart tugged. She really was a woman with all heart. It was as if he was doing a favor for her own child, instead of a client. She seemed really connected to her clients.

***

An hour later, Luke spent time with Jimmy on the ranch. Jimmy seemed to enjoy petting the horse, Randy. He seemed really connected. It melted Luke's heart when the boy smiled and laughed as he gave Randy some treats.

Later, they took a short trail ride while Jimmy sat on Randy. The therapist walked along with the horse to make sure the child was okay.

Horseback riding was not only fun for children with cerebral palsy, but it was also like a form of physical therapy. It was good for the child's physical and mental health.

Jemma had explained to Luke earlier that hippotherapy, as it was called, helped with physical, occupational, and sometimes speech therapy. She told him hippotherapy used the natural gait and movement of a horse to provide motor and sensory input for the child.

To say Luke was impressed with Jemma's knowledge of horse therapy was an understatement.

The easy breeze and the fresh air created a relaxing environment.

Jemma seemed to be enjoying herself just as much. He couldn't help but catch a glimpse of her beautiful silhouette as she rode out there with them on the trail. Her ebony hair and soft waves blowing in the wind. She looked like a model, only more down-to-earth. He loved the way she smiled and her infectious laughter as they made jokes going up the trail.

He felt so at ease like he had no other care in the world right now. He wasn't worried about work at the ranch—which he loved though it kept him busy from dawn to dusk, or the problems in the family, or the upcoming meetings he had to have with the lawyer dealing with his father's will. Being out there in the fresh air with Jemma and her client all seemed so magical—as if they were in a family together. It was as if he were somewhere else right now.

Paradise.

Yeah, right. This was only a gig. A client trail ride. Nothing more. He wasn't going to read too much into it. So what if this trail ride felt a lot different from all the other ones he'd been on?

Once in a while his brothers and he would take turns taking clients on trail rides, if time permitted, especially during special occasions like coming up to Christmas. His adoptive father always told him about the Christmas spirit.

Was this what it was all about? Maybe, he was getting caught up in the spirit of the season, that's all. Everyone got excited around this time of the year. But to him it was a reminder that he didn't have that kind of love in his life. Well, he was grateful for his adoptive family. They meant the world to him. And he loved activities like this, riding a horse trail with guests.

It was one of the fun activities on the ranch, all year round, as long as there was no snow on the ground and the conditions were safe.

Right now, he really had to keep his focus. The trail ride would be over soon, just like his time with Jemma.

***

"So, did you have a good time?" Sue Mae asked Luke later that day at the main house with a grin on her lips.

She stood in the kitchen as she checked on the roast in the oven.

Luke often visited the main house after working on the ranch. Then later he'd go home to his own cabin. Each brother occupied a cabin there. Each cabin was a home in itself with its own kitchen, dining facilities, three bedrooms each, a living room, and a fireplace.

In fact, he inhabited log cabin number one, near the main house, just a few steps away. Sue Mae moved into the main house when her brother Chet started getting weak after his wife passed. She was Chet's main caregiver at the end and took care of her brother.

Sue Mae never had a family of her own and was happy to take charge of the family and make sure everyone was all right. Sister Ellie also visited frequently and often stayed in a guest room at the main house.

Sometimes Luke would take turns cooking at the main house.

They had a cook, William, nicknamed Billy the Cook, on the premise for the lodge who also provided meals for the mess hall for all the ranch hands.

"A good time?" Luke replied, helping Sue Mae by taking the roast out of the oven.

"You know, with Jemma. Isn't she a sweetheart?"

Luke gave Sue Mae a sideways glance and arched his brow. "Sue Mae, what are you up to?"

"What makes you think I'm up to something, son?" Sue Mae said, with a wide grin.

"Okay, I know what's going on." Luke folded his arms across his chest. "Spill it out."

"Oh, come on now, Luke. You know you need to get married soon if you want to stay here. You and the boys."

"Oh, this again." Luke playfully rolled his eyes.

"Luke, I'm sorry about what your ex-wife did to you, but I'm sure you'll find the right woman..." Her voice trailed off. "Don't give up, Luke. That's probably why your father put that stipulation in the will. He knew deep down you believed in marriage and that there is someone out there for you."

Luke grabbed a bottle of water from the fridge, opened it, and took a sip.

He remembered how he felt when he proposed to his ex. How she'd taken his engagement ring and showed it off. Bragged to everyone. Made him feel as if she was devoted to him and only him. Meanwhile she'd played him like a game of chess. She stole his heart and robbed his spirit of happiness. And all this when he was serving in Afghanistan many years ago. He'd trusted his ex-wife. The further away he kept from love, the better. That almost killed him. It killed any dream of having love in his life forever.

"Why don't you ask Jemma to marry you?" Sue Mae just spilled it out like it was nothing.

Luke almost choked on his water. When was he going to learn to never drink anything around his aunt Sue Mae?

"What?" He coughed up.

Even the word marriage caused his spine to tingle with ice.

"Oh, dear. I notice you keep choking on your water, boy. You sure you don't have to have that checked out?"

"Sue Mae. The water's not the problem."

"The problem is you don't have much time," Sue Mae said. "Your father wanted to see you all happy and settled down."

"I know, I know. But you speak about Jemma like she's going to solve things. We've only just met. I don't know her. She doesn't know me. Why on earth would she want to marry me?"

"Because she...well, I'm not going to get into too much right now, but trust me, this arrangement would work in her favor too. Remember, I know everyone."

"You mean everyone's business, don't you?" Luke's grin was wide as he shook his head in disbelief. He loved his dear aunt, but sometimes he didn't know if she was coming or going.

"Luke, do you trust me?"

"Yes, of course I do. You know that, Sue Mae."

"Well, you must trust my judgement then. I'm a good judge of character. The only reason your last relationship didn't work out was because you didn't let me vet the woman first."

"Oh, come on now. You're not serious."

"Yes, of course I'm serious. I've managed to set up thirty couples at the church over the years who are still happily married. Why won't you boys let me arrange a marriage for you?"

"You really want me to answer that?"

"Besides, I don't want you boys having any regrets like I had."

"What do you mean?" Luke asked softly, seeing his adoptive aunt emotional.

"I never really told you boys the whole story before but..."

"But what?" His tone was gentle as he probed further.

"You remember I told you about my late husband?"

"Yes." Sorrow filled his heart for his aunt.

"Well, he served in Vietnam, just like my brother, your adoptive dad, Chet. And he didn't come back home."

His heart pulled. He knew the horrors of serving with friends overseas who never came home, except in a casket. It was gut wrenching.

"Well, I was so distraught. We were so young then. I was in my early twenties. Well, I vowed I'd never marry again."

Luke listened attentively, sadness overcame him.

"You see, I was so heartbroken and I turned down every man who tried to date me after years of being a young widow, grieving for my dear Tommy and grieving for the family we would never have. And I let that open window close. You see when a door closes, sometimes the Lord opens up a nice big bright window for us to go through, but if only we trusted Him more. Well, it got too late by the time I hit my sixties and now look at me in my eighties."

"Oh, Sue Mae. I'm really sorry about..."

"No, no. It's quite all right."

"But you know it's never too late," Luke offered. "I mean..."

"It's too late to have a family of my own, darling. Your dad was smart when he got married and found out he couldn't have children because of his injuries. He never let that stop him. He and Alanna adopted instead. And now they have you beautiful children to carry on. But I, on the other hand, was so crushed in spirit that I did not take up the opportunity to start again, Luke. I know you've been hurt badly, but please don't make my mistake. I think your father knew what he was doing by putting that stipulation in the will. He and I talked it over."

"You did?"

Talk about more secrets and revelations.

"Yes, and I agreed with him wholeheartedly. Give it a try. Jemma needs a spouse. *You* need a spouse. You just never know how it will work out in the end."

"I just don't want to make a mistake. I hardly know her. I mean even if she goes along with this marriage of convenience thing. What if we don't get along for the duration of…"

"I'd say at least six months to a year."

"Okay, six months to a year. That's a long time to be with someone under the same roof that you hardly know."

"She's good people. Trust me. I can tell a lot by a person. Besides, it's not just the way she carries herself. I've known her for many years."

"You have?"

"Yes, she's a good girl. She used to be in the church drama club. A fine actor, she was."

"Oh, boy. The last thing I need is an actor."

"Oh, no. Not that kind. She was a thespian at heart, but she was kind to the others. She never gossiped or backbite. She was thoughtful. And she takes really good care of her grandfather. He's not so well, you know."

"Sorry to hear that."

"Yes, well. She's at guest cabin number eight with the therapist and her client, Jimmy. She will be leaving soon. Why don't you stop by and say howdy?"

Chapter 6

Later that evening, Jemma's heart fluttered in her chest. Butterflies tickled her tummy. She couldn't remember the last time she'd felt that way. Ever.

Luke. Was. Hot.

Sure, he seemed serious most of the time as if he had the world on his shoulders, but there was something about him that resonated with her.

She'd never had a reaction like that to any man before. Not even with her ex when they'd first met. Luke was different. He was so...desirable.

And there was something about a cowboy that stirred all sorts of pleasant emotions inside her. Luke looked like a Christmas present, wrapped up in his red plaid shirt that showed his bulging biceps and muscular frame, that dark cowboy hat, belt buckle, and dark jeans with his cowboy boots. He was breathtaking. And she appreciated the way he tilted his cowboy hat when he first greeted her. So charismatic. And that voice! That deep sensuous voice swept her away.

But she had to brush those thoughts out of her mind. He might be one good-looking cowboy, but he was a man. And well, she was taking a long break from men right now.

The funny thing was she'd met Luke before, just not up close. This was when she was much younger, of course, when her grandfather brought her to the ranch to visit his good friend, Chet Carsen, Luke's now late father.

Jemma brought her thoughts back to the present as she sat in the living area of the guest cabin while the therapist stayed with Jimmy.

She wanted to touch base to see how he liked his session before leaving them. She was glad Jimmy's mother would be getting some much-needed respite while he stayed there with his therapist.

She wondered if she'd ever have children herself one day. It didn't look like it now. She wasn't exactly getting any younger. And she dreamed of being married. And that wasn't going to happen any time soon. Still, the work that she was doing filled her heart. Seeing kids like little Jimmy with a heart of gold, and a smile as wide as the ocean. That really made her day.

After saying her goodbyes to Jimmy and his nurse, Jemma made her way outside to her car parked outside the cabin.

When she got inside and fished for her car keys, she inserted the key to start the engine. But all she heard was the sound of an engine that was not going to cooperate.

"Oh, great."

The engine had died.

That's just what she needed. Could her life get any better?

Why was it that everything around her was dying? It felt as if the Christmas spirit was beginning to leave her too.

This was probably going to cost her more than she could afford. A trip to the garage, especially from a young lady who knew little about the mechanics of a car, was a mechanic's dream. They would probably find and charge her for all sorts of things wrong with the car.

How was she doing to drive and visit clients now and make trips with no car? And visits to the hospital, which was on the outskirts and far from transit.

She sat with her head on the steering wheel.

Where did she go wrong in her life?

A moment later, she was startled by a tap at the window.

It was that handsome cowboy, Luke.

She rolled down the window, surprised. It was early in the evening and the sun had begun to set. The beautiful hues highlighted Luke's handsome features. And he was handsome, stunning. She could not tear her gaze away from him.

"Hey Luke."

"Jemma, are you all right?"

"Well, could be better. My car won't start."

"Want me to look at that for you?"

"Sure. I'm so sorry to put you out like this."

"Hey, it's no worries at all."

When she unbuckled her seatbelt, she opened the car door. Luke held it open for her to come out. Their hands brushed slightly and oh, the sparks she felt traveled down her arms and to her belly. Butterflies exploded inside her.

What was that?

She wondered if he felt it too. She caught a whiff of his sweet cologne when he was inches from her. Or was that his aftershave?

For a moment, their eyes locked. She then tore her gaze from him and looked at the sunset.

"Beautiful, isn't it?" she said.

"Sure is," he said, his gaze stayed on her for a moment.

As if he caught himself, he looked off into the sunset too. "My dad used to love sitting on the porch of the main house there just watching the sunrise and the sunset. He said it gave him energy and hope for the new day. And appreciation for the day as it turned to night."

"Wow, he was right. It's so magical."

"You love it too?"

"Of course."

"Trouble is, people don't have much time anymore to just appreciate nature and the miracle of the universe. The sun being the source of energy and everything."

"I know. You're right. Sometimes we get so busy, we forget to stop and..." She was going to say smell the roses, but man, his sweet scent reminded her of her favorite spice. She wondered what cologne he was wearing but didn't want to ask him.

"You wanna watch the sun go down?" He spoke out of the blue and that stunned her.

She didn't know why. But the thing was, she wanted to. And she wanted to watch the sunset with *him* and she had no idea why. She hardly knew him. She only knew his family.

"Sure. I'd love that."

It wasn't as if she had anywhere to go right now. Her grandfather would be sleeping right now at the hospital, though she'd often stop by to make sure he'd taken his evening meds and she'd read to him while he fell asleep. But right now, she didn't have the ride to even get there. She'd just be going back to her lonely home on the east side.

"Good, I'll just check this beauty out here and find out what the trouble is."

He went into her car and started it. Sure enough the engine wouldn't start.

He adjusted his cowboy hat on his head. A nice sexy black cowboy hat. She admired his plaid shirt and his jeans. He fitted so well in his attire.

"I might have to make a call to get it to our garage."

"Oh, no. I can't ask you to do that," she said.

"Why not?" He looked genuinely puzzled. "My guys will have it up and running in no time. You don't trust me?" A smooth grin curved his lovely lips.

"Oh no, it's not that. It's just that...well, because I..."

The last thing Jemma wanted to sound was ungrateful or incoherent like she was now. What was with her? She normally had a bit more confidence than this. But around Luke, it all sort of melted away in the presence of his sweet southern charm and handsome features.

He was tall and handsome in every way. He intimidated her for some reason. It was the way he spoke in his thick southern accent and rich deep voice. So smooth and delicious, she could listen to him all day.

What was she going to say exactly?

She was the owner of *Jemma's Grant-A-Wish Foundation*, a successful online pairing company that paired ill children and adults with organizations that made their wishes come true. No one knew behind the scenes that she wasn't making any money off of it. It was a company close to her heart in many ways. But now that her grandfather was dying, she had other things on her mind like making sure his last days would be comfortable and filled with love. She hadn't thought any further about her future until now.

"Everything okay?"

"Oh, it's nothing. It's just that, well, you've been so kind already and I don't want to put you out."

"Hey, it's nothing. You're not putting me out, Jemma."

She loved the way he said Jemma. The words slid off his tongue like warm honey. So sweet, warm, and rich.

"You're our guest here," he continued. He then got out of the car and moved to the front and popped open the hood of the car with ease and started to look around.

"I think you're gonna need a new starter."

"A new starter? That sounds expensive. How much is that gonna cost?"

"Oh, don't worry about it." He paused for a moment as if thinking why would cost matter to her. Or was that her imagination?

"Oh no. It's really okay."

"You need to get it checked out, Jemma."

"I..."

"Listen, it's the Carsen way. I'd have it no other way. You're our guest and we take care of guests like family. No two ways about it."

She smiled warmly.

"Besides, your grandpa and Chet used to be best buddies. I'm sure he'd be unhappy if he thought we weren't going to help you out here."

"Okay, I can't argue with that."

She was grateful but felt a pang of guilt.

***

Moments later, after some men came to tow her car to their garage in town, he made good on his promise. They sat on the main porch and watched the beautiful sunset in the distance. It was magical. But being there with him was more so.

"I think it's great what you did back there with little Jimmy," Luke said to her.

"Hey, it's nothing. He deserves that. Thank you for making it happen, by the way."

"That's what we do here," Luke said. "What made you start up the company?"

"I was younger and well, my parents died in a crash..."

"Ah, man. I'm so sorry to hear that."

"It's all right. My grandfather was wonderful and adopted me. He pretty much raised me. That's why..."

"Why what?"

Oh, how much could she tell him? She really wanted to open up to Luke.

"You know you have this way about you that makes it easy to open up to you," she finally said. So much was weighing down on her right now and she wanted to open up.

"I do?" He sounded surprised, but there was a sweet grin on his lips.

"Yeah, hasn't anyone ever told you before?"

His expression changed. "My ex-wife."

"Your ex-wife?"

"It's a long story."

"Oh, one of those, huh?"

"Yeah, you could say that."

Later, after they talked and watched the sunset together, Luke took her home in his blue Ford pickup truck. It was a nice truck. They enjoyed the evening, talking about all sorts of things. She couldn't believe how much they had in common. It was surreal. She didn't remember when she last had such a good conversation about all sorts of things. His brother did the rodeo circuit a while back. He told her about how they moved back to help his father with the ranch.

She was impressed at how warm and friendly they all were. He'd introduced her to them earlier. What a close-knit tight family they were. She'd never seen such an animated group before. They joked and teased each other. It was evident they took great care of the ranch and took turns managing each aspect, but they also knew how to have fun. She noticed that none of them wore a wedding band. They were all good looking, tall, handsome, and hard-working cowboys with great personalities. Yet, they hid out there on the ranch focusing on nothing but that.

She felt like part of a big family being there. She loved the way they all jumped in to help her out. She'd never known what that was like before, having a big family. She was an only child and her grandmother had passed when she was young. So when her parents went to be with the Lord, it was always just her and her grandfather.

Her heart sank, thinking about how close it was to Christmas time. He might not live to see past Christmas, or to see his only beloved granddaughter married and carry on his family legacy.

She swallowed hard as he walked her up to the front steps of her home.

"Thanks for taking me home."

"No trouble, Jemma. Just call me if you need anything."

"I will. And I guess I'll see you tomorrow then."

"Tomorrow?" He looked puzzled.

"Yes, remember Jimmy will be spending the week there."

"Yeah, I know that. We have a lot of fun things planned for him."

"I'll be there to make sure everything's good. I'm sure it will be, but that was part of the arrangement."

Was that her imagination or did a grin curve the corner of his beautiful lips.

"Sure. I guess, I can handle that."

She grinned.

He then watched her go inside the house to make sure she was safe. She appreciated his chivalry and was glad it was still alive and well in today's society.

She waved him on.

He waved her on and then he left and rode away. Out of her life. For now.

When she got inside, she caught her breath.

Earlier, she noticed he'd glanced at her hands. Was he interested in finding out if she was dating or seeing anyone or perhaps engaged? But then he would probably already know that, wouldn't he? She thought it was strange that his aunt Sue Mae insisted they get together.

There was something up. She just couldn't put her finger on it. Should she have said anything about it? But then she didn't want to embarrass herself.

She picked up the phone to call the hospital to check on her grandfather.

"Yes, he had a quiet evening," the nurse said. "But he kept talking about a Christmas wedding."

"A Christmas wedding?" Jemma asked, puzzled.

"Yes, he kept saying how he wished he could have seen you happily married before he goes to be with the Lord—before Christmas. He says he wants you to be happy."

Jemma's heart crushed inside her.

"He said that?" She swallowed hard.

"Yes, it's all he kept talking about Jemma. I'm sorry to have to tell you that."

"Oh, no. Like I said, I need to know everything. I'll be there first thing in the morning." Jemma hung up the phone, dazed.

Sure, she'd just met a sweet guy tonight. A true cowboy with all heart, as far as she could tell, but there was no way she could fulfill her grandfather's wish of getting married by Christmas. Even if she were to fake it.

Luke would think she was crazy.

But right now, she was dying inside thinking about her grandfather's last wish. The man who made all her wishes come true and gave her a second chance at life said he only wanted to see her happy because getting married was all she ever spoke about, all she ever dreamed about—until her ex broke her heart.

Could she ever grant him that one last wish to see her happily married?

Chapter 7

A week later, Luke returned from the feed and ranch supply store and hurled the sacks of feed off the truck.

His thoughts kept travelling back to sweet Jemma. She was stunning. And those lips of hers. He wondered what they'd feel like, taste like. That's if he ever got a chance to kiss her. But no way was that ever gonna happen. Still, he could dream about it, couldn't he? The thought of her caused butterflies to flutter in his stomach. No woman had ever had that kind of effect on him before.

A moment later, his brothers Beau and Jesse walked over to help.

"Luke, you have a skip in your step, bro," Beau said to Luke, helping him with the supplies.

"You talking to me?" Luke said.

"You know what I mean. That girl. What's her name? Jemma, right?"

"What about her?"

"Come on now, don't tell me you haven't noticed a change."

"Nope."

"What Beau's saying is that you haven't been yourself this past week," Jesse chimed in.

"And that's good, because you ain't all that." Beau loved to tease Luke.

"Right back at you, bro." Luke grinned.

"You thinking of asking her out?" Beau asked.

"We made a pact, Beau," Jesse added. "You know he's not getting involved again.

"But what about Dad's will and the agreement to stay here?" Beau said.

"Okay, boys. You're getting ahead of yourself," Luke replied. "I just met her."

"You know a lot about her."

"Not to mention Sue Mae was talking earlier this week about how much she knows Jemma. She said you two would be a great match."

Luke sighed to himself. "Yeah, so would my boots and jacket. Doesn't mean I'm gonna get into this fake marriage business."

"But you both seem to really connect. Haven't seen you around anyone like that before. You were all smiling from ear-to-ear, bro. Can't top that."

"What's that supposed to mean?" Luke said.

"If we really have to go through with this and get hitched to stay here to save our family's ranch, wouldn't you rather be with someone you can tolerate being around?" Beau arched his brow.

Luke knew Beau had a point. He just didn't want to admit it to his brother right now, lest his brother's head swells so much that his cowboy hat would no longer fit. But silently Luke pondered Beau's words.

Moments later, after he'd gotten all the feed sacks off the truck with his brothers, Luke was left to himself again. And to his thoughts.

Should he ask Ms. Jemma out? His aunt knew Jemma very well and Jemma *was* a friend of the family.

Truth be told, he'd had one heck of a week with Jemma and her client Jimmy.

They'd spent time on the ranch, on the horse trail, petting the horses, taking a tour of the facilities, watching sunsets before he took her home. Her car was still at the garage and she'd be picking it up soon. She even insisted on taking him to lunch since he wouldn't let her pay for the repairs. But he couldn't let her do that. He was always raised to treat a lady, not have it the other way round.

They had gone out to lunch in town and had a good time, but he'd insisted on paying for the lunch and he did.

Still, he had to keep a focus. It was one thing for marriage, but he vowed he'd never give his heart to another woman ever again. He just couldn't.

He'd never felt this way about his ex-wife, although he *did* love his ex and thought she'd always be there for him, with him. But that went sour fast, didn't it?

His brothers had kept telling him he was different around Jemma, whatever that meant. He denied it, of course.

Every day during the past week when he'd seen Jemma and spent time with her and Jimmy for the boy's week-long stay at the ranch, they'd gone out for lunch.

The boy enjoyed the hen house and chasing Cocoa, their border collie.

He'd enjoyed his time with them...It reminded him of what he'd been missing out on having a family of his own to protect, to take care of, to have fun with.

Sure, he had that with his brothers, but this was a little different. That's what he'd wanted with his ex-wife and she'd crushed that dream of his with her betrayal and leaving him for another man, his friend, and having another man's child.

The thought burned into his heart. How could she hurt him like that?

Nope, he'd never fall in love again. Not that he was falling for Jemma. He'd give it a thought. But the trouble was, would Jemma even go for it?

His aunt seemed to think so.

Sue Mae kept saying that Jemma was in search of a husband, but Jemma didn't seem to act like it. She never once brought it up. She only spoke to him briefly about her ex breaking her heart and that was that. She was focused on her business, her grandfather and helping others.

Could Sue Mae have gotten it wrong?

An hour later, he heard a car pulling up to the side. It was Jemma in her silver sedan.

"Hey, Jemma."

"Luke, how are you doing?"

"Good. You?"

"Very good. I can't thank you enough for what you did for me. I wish you'd let me treat you."

The words slid through him with delight. She had no idea how much she'd already done for him.

It's true, he was a different person around her. He loved her spirit. Her kind words. The way she said his name and looked into his eyes. He'd never gotten any of that from his ex-wife. He even loved the fact that Jemma and he shared the same interests.

His other brothers never understood what it meant to watch the sunsets and sunrises on the ranch. Jemma did though. She never teased him about it or said he was wasting his time. She got him. She understood him.

Wait a minute, Luke. Don't fall for her. Remember, love and you just don't mix well.

"Listen, I insist on taking you out to lunch or dinner or something," she persisted again.

He took a good look at her car. "Sounds good."

"Lunch?"

"No, the engine. Glad they did a good job on it."

She grinned.

"I'm just teasing. Sure, let's have lunch, but it's my treat, Jemma." He gave her a warm smile.

Later, they sat at a restaurant in town.

"So, how's little Jimmy doing?" he asked.

"He's good. Thanks for asking. He had the most amazing time this past week. I can't thank you enough. You guys are so amazing here—you made his wish come true."

"Glad to hear it. Although you're the one who made his wish come true." He felt warm inside from her words.

He could tell she was genuine about helping others and making sure her clients were happy.

"Wanna catch the lighting of the Christmas tree in the town square, later?" he asked her.

"I'd love that. Yes, later. I'll meet you there."

***

Later that afternoon, after they watched the lighting on the Christmas tree in the Sweet Rivers Town Square and sang

Christmas carols, Luke and Jemma walked towards the Sweet Rivers Café in town.

"This is wonderful."

"Yes, it is."

"I wish it could be Christmas all year round," she said, dreamily.

"Why?"

"Because there's just something magical about this time. Miracles happen, dreams come true, family comes first—this all is about the birth of Christ and His love in the world. It's a reminder that we need to give that gift of love and happiness to others. There's no other feeling like it. Everyone recognizes it, even if they don't know it at first."

He was touched by her words. But was there such a thing as the Christmas spirit? He'd lost a lot of faith in humanity over the past few years, especially after what his ex-wife did to him.

"Yes, it's important to remember that," was all he said.

Christmas songs played over the sound speakers at the market, everyone was jolly and festive and laughing and chatting to each other. The place was alive.

She was right. There was nothing sweeter than the spirit of the Christmas season.

Speaking of which, the Christmas spirit was a true thing. He knew it. And it prompted him to make it happen.

What did he have to lose? Except maybe she'd turn him down cold and think he'd lost his marbles somewhere.

He was going to ask her to marry him. He was going to make his father happy up there in heaven. And do right by the family ranch. Even if it wasn't a real marriage, so to speak. What could it hurt?

Man, even thinking about it gave his stomach a good tension squeeze.

Maybe he should just forget about it.

Chapter 8

Jemma felt a warm glow through her body as she sat in front of Luke Carsen. She'd enjoyed every moment with him this past week. He was so easy to get along with. He always said the sweetest things to her. She'd never had that with her ex, funnily enough. She couldn't even recount any sweet moments with Thomas.

But right now, she had other things on her mind. Like honoring her grandfather's last wish. And how she felt about Luke.

They sat at the Sweet Rivers Café with their order of hot chocolates with cinnamon-flavored candy canes, marshmallows, and whipped cream.

"How's your grandpa doing today?" Luke asked, a concerned expression on his face.

Luke had been so sweet to ask her every time he saw her how her grandfather was doing. And it wasn't just a casual how's-he-doing. It was more of a how's-he-really-doing,-I-want-to-know-I-really-care type of thing.

"I just saw him again this morning." Tears pricked her eyes. "I see him every day, but..."

"Are you okay?"

She nodded slowly. Though she was feeling anything but okay. It was hard to explain to anyone, especially to Luke about her grandfather's last wish.

"It's just that...well, we spoke about the time he has left, and I just want to spend each second with him, every single day."

"I understand."

"It's not just that. He...when I'm there he tells me how sorry he is that..."

Just then her cell phone rang. It was probably for the best. Saved by the ring.

She was about to spill it all out to Luke about how her grandfather hoped she'd be married by Christmas before he passed on. But that's an impossible dream, an impossible wish. She knew it and it broke her heart.

Even if she found someone, she didn't trust herself around them. After her ex's mental abuse, she didn't know if she could trust her judgement anymore.

That was it. Plain and simple. She'd have to find another way, somehow, to make her grandfather happy in his last days. But she just couldn't do that.

When she glanced at the screen of her phone, she saw that it was a call from an unknown number.

"Sorry, I should probably take this." She bit down on her lower lip when she spoke to him.

"No problem."

"Hello?" she asked cautiously. There was no one on the other end of the phone line. She then looked up and then grinned and shook her head. She listened for a moment as Luke watched her cautiously with a slight concern on his face.

She decided not to speak again, knowing there were a lot of phone scams out there where the caller might want to record your voice for various nefarious reasons including using it as a voice-authentication duplication to get into secured accounts. It was all too crazy, but it was better to be cautious than careless. If it were a true business, they'd have said something by now. They'd have asked for her, even if they didn't hear a sound.

She hung up.

Of course, it could just be dead air. Maybe it was just a misdial. But from an unknown number? She'd had a few of those calls lately.

Right, that settled it. It was a sign from above. She was not to tell Luke about her dilemma and her father's last wish. If that wasn't a clear sign, she didn't know what was. Of course, she could be wrong. But still, she decided to change the subject.

"Wrong number?" Luke asked, gently.

"Probably," she said. Or maybe it was the right number—at the right time.

Later, they placed their orders and enjoyed Texas-style lasagna with side servings of picante sauce, guacamole and tortilla chips and fresh garden vegetables.

It was funny how they enjoyed the same type of foods.

After the café, they walked out into the parking lot. Luke walked her to her car. He paused for a moment. The sky was changing colors again for the evening. A beautiful hue of reds and oranges streaked the darkening blue evening sky.

"You thinking what I'm thinking?" He arched his brow with a grin.

"I think so."

They drove to the ranch and sat on the porch watching the sunset in the distance. His porch seemed to have the best view of the sunset with the miles of rolling pastures in the distance. The mood was serene. Breathtaking. Maybe the Lord wanted her to have this time to regroup and unwind after her tensions and to help ease the weight off her shoulders. She needed this time to take a breath. To slow down her racing mind. To enjoy the beauty of nature for a change. To still her worries.

"Thanks for spending this time with me. I enjoy your company," Luke said.

"Me too. I can't believe how breathtaking the sunsets are out here. You must have the best view in Sweet Rivers."

He grinned.

"My dad used to watch it every night, no matter what."

"Must have helped. He lived long and worked on the ranch while he was in his senior years."

Luke paused for a moment.

"Something's wrong." It was more of a statement, an observation than a question.

"I guess you could say that," he said.

"Penny for your thoughts."

"My father's will was read recently."

"Oh?"

"Yeah, I know, it's been a year now since he passed just before Christmas."

"I'm so sorry to hear that. It must have been difficult for you, especially around this time of the year."

"Yeah, it sure was," he said, his eyes filled with sadness. "He was a true believer in all things love."

"Unlike you," she said, arching her brow now.

"What makes you think that?"

"Well, you've been hurt before. And trust me, I can relate. So you don't share his views on it, am I right?"

"Yeah, but recently I've been thinking about marriage."

"What?" She was stunned now.

"Oh, no. It's not like it sounds."

Luke explained everything about Chet Carsen's will and the conditions of it and the ranch.

"Oh, Luke, I don't know what to say. That's...wow...that's difficult."

"It sure is."

"What are you going to do?"

"Get married."

"Get married?" She bit down on her lower lip. Her heart galloped in her chest. "Have you thought of anyone?"

"Yes. You."

Jemma froze.

Chapter 9

Luke could kick himself.

What was he thinking? Or what was he *drinking*?

Asking Jemma like that? Asking that poor girl to marry him? He was half expecting her to make a run for it now. But she just sat there, frozen to the spot. Probably in shock, poor thing.

There must have been something in the water. Or was it the Christmas spirit taking over, causing him to just spill out his thoughts?

Aw, man. What had he done?

"Jemma, are you okay? Sorry, I didn't mean to spring that on you like that. I was just kidding."

"You were?" She turned to him, surprised.

Was that the look of disappointment on her face? Disappointment that he wasn't going to ask her to marry him? Or that he'd asked her in the first place? Right about now, he just couldn't tell.

"I mean..." Now Luke was fumbling for words.

Luke never fumbled for words. He was always in control. But around Jemma, there was just something in him that changed. He was like warm butter melted in a pan on the stove.

"Look, I guess your aunt, Sue Mae, told you about my grandfather's dying wish."

"Wait. What?" Now it was Luke's turn to be stunned into silence.

"She didn't tell you?" Jemma looked genuinely surprised.

Now, just what on earth was going on there? It was as if they were in some sort of alternate universe.

"Tell me what?" He adjusted his black cowboy hat on his head.

"Oh, no." She got up, looking flustered. She felt around in her purse for her car keys. "Never mind. I think this is just one big mistake. I'd better be going."

"Now wait a minute there, Jemma. You were gonna say something. Are you all right? I don't want you leaving like this."

She paused for a moment, looking up at the beautiful sunset in the sky, then she turned her gaze back to him.

She was magnificent in every sense of the word.

The warm glow of the sun highlighted her beautiful high cheekbones and soft-looking lips and her large brown cinnamon-colored eyes. She was gorgeous.

He'd never seen a woman as beautiful as her before. And it was more than just her exterior beauty. That beautiful soul of hers resonated with him. But he had to focus right now. There were more matters he had to deal with.

Was it something he said? Okay, fool, of course it was something he said. He just asked a perfect stranger to marry him. Well, almost a perfect stranger. She was perfect, but she wasn't exactly a stranger.

Jemma sat back down. She put her hands in her hair then she covered her face with her hands. She took in a deep breath as if to compose herself then she spilled it all out. Everything that was in her heart.

"Oh, Jemma. I'm really sorry to hear that. I had no idea," Luke said, after Jemma told him her dilemma.

"You mean Sue Mae didn't say anything to you about that?" She didn't seem too convinced, and he was an honest man. He'd tell her the truth.

"She told me that you were looking for a husband and given my situation here at the ranch she thought we should give it a go. But she never went into any details about your grandfather's condition and his last wishes for you to get married, hopefully by Christmas. I had no idea. It must be really hard for you."

"Yes, it is," she said, dazed. "I wish I could make it happen for him. He knows that being happily married has always been my dream. He wants to see me happy. I'm able to make everyone else's dreams come true."

"You can make his dream come true. And I can fulfill my father's last wishes in his will too. It'll be a win-win situation."

She looked up and gazed into his eyes.

He adjusted his cowboy hat again.

"It sounds good in theory," Jemma said.

"But..." Luke said, softly, cuing her on.

"I was engaged to be married before, but he lied to me. I don't think I can ever trust another man again, Luke."

"Now, that's not fair. To you, I mean. Just 'cause your ex was a real piece of work, don't let him stop you from finding happiness."

"Like you?" she said. "You yourself said you weren't looking to ever get married again."

"Okay, I did say that. But this wouldn't be a real marriage. It would be a business arrangement. That would be different, right?"

"I guess." She looked thoughtfully.

"We just wouldn't tell anyone what we're doing, outside of the family, I mean. And you can stay here at the ranch. There's plenty of room here. Lots of cabins."

"But we'd have to at least share the same cabin."

"Yes. We could share cabin number one. It's a three-bedroom log cabin. Got a fireplace and everything. Large kitchen and living room space. We'd sleep in separate rooms, of course."

"Of course." She swallowed so hard, he thought he saw a lump go down in her throat. Was she going to do this? Would she go along with this?

"It would work out for the both of us. We could visit your grandpa at the hospital and show him the ring. We could even have a ceremony out there or here at the ranch and have him brought down here to witness it. It would make his heart sing."

She thought about it for a moment.

"Luke, it all sounds great. Too good to be true, but..."

"But what?"

Tears filled her beautiful brown eyes. "You're a sweet guy, Luke. You really are, but...I can't do this. I'm so sorry."

"I thought this is what you wanted?" His voice was soft.

"I do., but...I don't want to make a terrible mistake. I mean, after the wedding...then what? I always dreamed that if I took my vows, it would be for real. Not some game."

"It's not a game. It's a marriage of convenience. They're more common than you think."

He was about to tell her what his aunt had told him how sometimes marriages start off with love and end up being one of convenience and vice-versa, but he didn't want to scare her off.

He couldn't see how she couldn't see the win-win situation. On the other hand, she was right. They would be in front of a preacher saying their vows.

"Just think about it, okay?"

"Okay," she sighed deeply. "It all sounds so good in theory, but then there's practice. I'll give it a thought and let you know my answer by the end of the week."

Why did he get the feeling she was going to say forget it?

Chapter 10

Later that night, Jemma tossed and turned in her bed. Why was it that it always took her forever to fall asleep?

Was it because she had so much on her mind? She read somewhere that if you were unable to turn off your thoughts it might keep your brain too active to fall into that sleep mode.

Well, she really had to get her mind off her troubles right now.

She could not believe Luke Carsen asked her to marry him.

A wide grin perched on her lips, but then it was soon replaced with a frown. She held onto her pillow as she thought about it.

He wanted to enter into an arranged marriage of convenience so that he could fulfill his father's last wish to be a married family man on the family ranch.

She didn't know if she should feel flattered or insulted.

But then again, she wanted him too. She needed a groom to make her dear grandfather's dying wish come true, didn't she?

But Luke had asked her to marry him before he knew about her grandfather's situation. What was she to make of that?

She fluffed the pillow then placed it back down on the bed as if that would help her to sleep better.

She then got up out of bed and slipped into her slippers. It was cold in the house, so she reached for her dressing gown. She had to get some sleep, or she'd be toast. Her nerves would be all over the place. Sleep was the way the body got rest and repaired itself, helped a person rejuvenate for the next day. She could not afford to skip out on sleep.

She remembered that sweet electrical current that passed through her yesterday as Luke brushed her skin. And that sweet southern charm of his. She loved everything about him. But it would be all wrong.

What would happen after they got married?

Would they just remain in a loveless fake marriage for goodness knew how long?

Nope.

She just couldn't do it. There was no way she could go through with it. Whenever she said her vows, if that ever happened, it was going to be for real or it wouldn't happen.

She went into the kitchen and glanced at the clock on the wall. It read 4:00 a.m. Her grandfather had bought that old antique clock many years ago. She remembered that old clock growing up. It was part of the family. She hated that she'd have to move from this house soon, especially after her grandfather...

She tried not to think about that right now.

Her mind did, however, trail on Luke Carsen. She wondered if he'd be up soon. He told her he woke up between 4:30 a.m. and 5:00 a.m. every morning to get things going on the ranch. He told her he loved the early morning time, rising before the sunrise or catching the sun peak over the horizon first thing in the morning.

She thought about how dreamy life would be on the ranch, married to a rancher. But only if it were a real marriage.

She fixed herself some tea and then went over to the sofa. She picked up one of her romance novels from the bookshelf, it was a book by one of her favorite authors C. C. Dale. That woman could write like there was no tomorrow. Maybe a bit of pick-me-up would help her right now. She could read for a half hour or so then maybe she'd fall asleep with hopeful thoughts on her mind, instead of her worries and then that would help her to fall asleep.

Before long, as she dove into the first chapter, the phone rang.

"Who could be calling at this time of the morning?" she said out loud.

Jemma reached over to pick up the phone. But stopped when she saw it was the Sweet Rivers Hospital calling.

At 4:15 in the morning?

This was *not* a good sign.

Chapter 11

During last night, Luke could hardly sleep. He got up before the alarm clock sounded at 5:00 a.m. He kept thinking about sweet Jemma all night. He was sure he dreamt about her, but he couldn't remember.

There was just something about Jemma that resonated with his soul. Not that he'd ever commit again to another woman, but he could at least be friends with her, couldn't he?

He really hoped she'd take him up on his offer and accept his proposal. After all, it would work out for both of their benefit, wouldn't it?

Moments later, Luke was out on the field. He backed up his tractor to pick up a bale of hay. Then later, he unspooled the bale of hay using the spooler to spread the hay out for the cows. As he laid out a row of hay, the cows gathered around to feed.

It gave him joy to see the cattle taken care of. The Carsens took great care of their livestock and made sure they were well fed, healthy and had a whole lot of room to graze when needed.

Later that morning, he found himself back at the ranch main house. His brother, Beau walked into the common area after fixing some of the fences.

"Are you okay?" Beau asked.

"Course, why?"

"Come on, bro. I know you. Something happened, didn't it?"

"Nothing happened."

"What happened? She changed her mind?" Beau probed.

He gave his brother a look. "I asked her to marry me."

"You did? So you went through with it? What did she say?"

"She said she'd think about it."

"Aw, man. Sorry about that."

"Sorry about what? She didn't say no."

"But she didn't say yes, either. You know the more I think about this, the more I think Chet had the right heart, but in reality, this thing's not gonna work. We need to contest the will."

"I don't think that's an option," Luke said.

"Why not?"

"Because didn't Joe say that anyone who contests the will gets nothing? Meaning no part of this ranch."

"I must have missed that part."

"Sure looks like it."

"You know as much as I do, this ranch is everything to the family. Why can't they just see that we want to live for the land?"

Luke knew how his brother felt.

Beau had been in a similar situation to Luke. Beau's wife had been cheating on him too, but she sadly died in an accident—with her lover. It nearly knocked Beau out of his mind. As much as his wife had cheated on him, he still loved her. But after that, he vowed he'd never marry again. Luke could relate to that sentiment.

"Beau, there just isn't any way around it." The thought crushed Luke's spirit.

What if Jemma said no?

What if she didn't need to be in a marriage of convenience as much as he did?

Then what?

He couldn't bear the thought of losing the Sweet Rivers Family Ranch. It would kill him. He felt as if he was one with the land, with the spirit of the place, and with nature. The beauty of the ranch made his heart skip with joy every morning he woke up before the sunrise.

It sure gave him a renewed sense of purpose when he returned to Texas, after he left the big city to move back to the ranch.

It had been a blessing in disguise when his aunt called him that day years ago to tell him and his brothers that their adoptive father Chet wasn't getting any younger and as much as he loved working on the land, he needed help.

They were all more than willing to come back and help save the family ranch and help the man who'd adopted them. Chet would've been too proud to call himself. He'd rejected the idea at first but then he came around to the reality that he was getting old, and he wasn't as energetic and strong as he once was.

Did he learn this denial thing from his adoptive father?

For a long time Luke had thought he didn't need anyone. Especially after his ex-wife broke his heart and crushed his spirit with that gut wrenching text message she'd meant for another man, admitting she'd cheated on him and was having someone else's child while he was serving in Afghanistan years ago.

But now, he was beginning to have second thoughts about things.

He knew he couldn't love that way again, but he could at least try the companionship marriage of convenience thing, couldn't he?

What harm could that do?

But he still needed a bride. And soon.

Trouble was, Jemma was someone he could tolerate being around at least, but he had a sick feeling inside the pit of his soul that she was going to say no.

If she wanted to say yes, she would have done it already, wouldn't she? She probably just wanted to let him down easily over the phone.

"I gave her until the end of the week to make up her mind," Luke said to his brother.

"And what if she says no?"

"Then I'll have to figure out the next step after that."

"Right."

"And what about you? Have you thought of anyone?" Luke asked.

"Nope. I don't know what I'm gonna do because marriage and I don't mix. Been there done that. Not going down that lonely country road again."

"This is just great, isn't it? Look at us. You know the lawyer and Sue Mae's not going to let us live this down."

"I know that. But right now, you've got to think about Jemma. I have to admit, as much as I don't believe in marriage again, you two do seem to really click. I can feel that energy around you two. There's just something about you when you're with her."

Luke felt warm inside. He knew his brother was telling the truth, but still, if she said yes, it would be in name only. And that's a big *if.* He pulled out his cell phone from his pocket and glanced at the screen, thinking he might have missed her call.

Nope. No phone calls.

He'd give her some time.

He sure hoped she'd go along with this marriage of convenience. If not for his sake, then for *her* sake.

Chapter 12

Jemma couldn't breathe. She tried to suck in a deep breath. At the hospital she held onto her grandfather's hand. His hand was cold. Just as cold as she felt inside right now. How could this be?

The room was beautifully decorated in Christmas decorations reminding her of this special time of the year. But right now, it felt like the most heart-breaking time of the year for her. She'd forever remember this memory.

"He's holding on," Nurse Jackson, the nurse in the room, told Jemma, softly.

"Holding on?" Jemma whispered as her grandfather lay in the bed, still as ice, his breath as slow as molasses.

"Yes, he's hoping to see you happy," she said. "That's what he told us. He's so worried about you being alone when he's gone," the nurse continued.

"Oh, Jemma, darling," Grandpa turned to her. His eyes half open. "I really wanted to see you settle down. I prayed that I'd see you happy and married before I go to be with the Lord. But I guess we can't always have what..."

"Oh, Grandpa..." Her heart squeezed in her chest. "You'll see me married."

He opened his eyes a little wider with surprise. "What did you say, darling?"

"I...uh...I was going to surprise you...I...I'm getting married and well, soon..."

What. Just. Happened?

What did she just say? Was she going insane?

It was as if a light of hope shone across her grandfather's face. A magical spirit circled around him.

Jemma could feel it through the energy in his hands.

"Grandpa?"

He propped himself up on the bed as if he'd gotten new light—renewed strength.

"You're getting married?" His face brightened with a small curve of his lips.

"Well, uh..." *Oh, please forgive me, Lord.* "Yes."

She bit down on her lower lip, hoping he wouldn't notice there was something she was hiding. Like the fact that she'd contemplated entering into a marriage of convenience.

Well, it wasn't exactly a lie now, was it? Luke Carsen did in fact ask her to marry him.

"Oh, darling," he said, his voice groggy from fatigue. "Darling, you have no idea how happy that makes me feel knowing that you'll have what you always wanted."

"Congratulations!" Nurse Jackson said.

"Excuse me?" Jemma said.

"About your engagement. Congratulations."

"Oh...uh, yes, right. Thank you."

Oh, no. Could she keep this up? What was she thinking? Oh, great. Now all she had to do was convince Luke to marry her—*this week!*

Was that going to happen?

So she had to go through with it now, didn't she?

But what if Luke changed his mind? She wasn't exactly warm and fuzzy with him about the whole notion. She'd made it clear to Luke that she'd only get married if it were a real marriage, not a fake one. It looked as if everything was not going to go as she'd originally planned.

"I'm so happy, darling," her grandfather said again, tears of joys streaming down his face. "Oh, thank you, Lord." His voice was warm and filled with hope.

How could Jemma take that joy away from him?

The one man who'd been there for her all her life growing up without her parents. He'd given her so much and asked for nothing in return except for her to be happy.

She looked up at the nurse and saw her dab her own eyes too. Everyone was filled with emotion in the room. And truth be told, so was Jemma, in a way. If only her marriage would be a real one. But that still left an untied piece of string.

The groom.

He had yet to be notified.

"So who is this lucky fella?" Grandpa asked.

"Uh...Luke Carsen."

Grandpa eyed Jemma with surprise. "*Luke Carsen*? Chet Carsen's boy?"

"Yes, his adopted son." Jemma gave a nervous chuckle.

Jemma's insides squeezed hard.

Oh, boy. She was really in for it now.

What if he contacted anyone to do with the Carsens? But then again, who would he speak to? Maybe Pastor Dave from the church.

Oh, no. Oh, no. Oh, no.

She had to call Luke quick to let him know her answer! Or the whole thing would fall apart like a crumpled biscuit.

She glanced down at her watch then back to Grandpa. She really needed to call Luke and let him know she wanted to go ahead with the marriage and sooner than planned.

Would he go through with it?

Oh no. What if he was busy? What if he had other plans this week?

"I want to be there," Grandpa said, proudly.

"Oh, of course, Grandpa. But would you be strong enough to attend?"

"Nonsense." Her grandfather spoke with confidence. "Nurse, you think we could arrange this? I need to be there for my only grandchild's wedding. I can't miss it for the world. I need a suit. I need to get a good suit."

The nurse smiled. "One step at a time, Mr. Smith. We need to let the doctor know first. Remember, the doc said you may not be strong enough to leave the facility."

"Well, we can do it here, can't we? Didn't Chuck say his vows down the hall?"

"That's true."

Jemma remembered one of the eighty-year-old residents married his long-time love—both of them were widowed and wanted to say their vows there. It was a lovely occasion. So heart-warming, beautiful. The staff had gone to great lengths to make it a magical experience for them. They brought in a pastor from one of the churches nearby since the chaplain wasn't available at the time and decorated the little chapel at the hospital long-term care wing with gorgeous floral arrangements.

Could they do that for Jemma and Luke?

She glanced around at the Christmas decorations. So breathtaking. They'd be nothing like a Christmas wedding, sort of like an enchanted winter wonderland theme.

But she was getting way ahead of herself and she knew it.

"What's wrong, darling? You look nervous. You've been looking at your phone every minute. Got an appointment?"

"Uh...yes, Grandpa. I...uh...I have to make an urgent call." *To my groom-to-be to inform him that he's going to be...a groom.*

"Well, don't let me stop you, darling."

"We can arrange for Friday if you wish," the nurse said. "I could speak with the doctor."

That was a few days away.

Could she really get married in less than a week?

What about Luke? What would his plans look like? What if he changed his mind?

"Uh...sure...let me just check it over with Luke."

"Of course."

She knew her grandfather's condition was deteriorating. His prognosis was so unfavorable. Her skin prickled with heat. She had to do this now and fast.

Moments later, she tried Luke's phone number for the tenth time. It rang for a while and then went straight to voicemail—again. She saw her phone battery level was only at 5%—about the same level as her patience right now. She'd forgotten to charge it yesterday after all that happened.

Oh, why won't Luke answer his phone?

Was he busy on the ranch? Probably.

He clearly had tons of work to do, and she made it clear she'd get back to him next week. Not now.

Did he change his mind? Oh, she hoped not. That would ruin everything. Not to mention her grandfather's heart would be smashed to pieces. She couldn't let that happen.

"Hey, Luke, it's Jemma." She spoke into the phone. "Please call me as soon as you get this message."

She didn't want to sound too desperate, but she needed him to know it was urgent.

She had a sick feeling in the pit of her stomach that Luke had changed his mind about this whole fake marriage thing.

Chapter 13

Luke just saw the missed calls from Jemma's number when he returned to his cabin and tried to call her back immediately.

There was no answer.

Darn it.

He saw that she'd tried to call his number about a dozen times, back-to-back. Was she all right? He hoped she wasn't stranded somewhere or had an emergency.

He glanced at the side of his phone and realized his phone ringer was still turned to silence. He often turned off the ringer late at night so he could get a restful night sleep. He knew that if there was an emergency he could be reached on the landline phone in the house which also sat by his night table. He was one of those people who still used a landline phone *and* a cell phone.

He should have given Jemma his house number. Why hadn't he thought of that before?

His mind had all sorts of thoughts running through it, including thoughts of Jemma and what her lips would feel like when they kissed on their wedding day, *if* she said yes to his marriage proposal, of course.

But then another thought slid into his mind. His ex-wife and what she'd done to his heart.

He was beginning to have doubts about pulling off this marriage of convenience thing.

He was so torn with what to do about his adoptive father's last wishes from his will.

His mind was packed by the time he rose this morning. It was as if he was going on autopilot when doing his morning errands on the ranch.

That's probably why he'd forgotten to turn on his phone.

Maybe subconsciously, he wanted to do that so he wouldn't have to deal with a rejection from Jemma.

But who was he kidding?

He was still haunted over that text message from his now ex-wife, the one she'd meant for her lover but instead the message went to his phone.

He felt a gut-wrenching blow to his stomach over the memory of that day. A day forever etched in his soul and in his heart.

But that was then, he had to let go of the past in order to move forward, as his old man would tell him.

Luke tried calling Jemma again as he looked out from his window where he got a good view of the land. The sky was blue with a slight overcast in the distance of dark clouds. It was probably going to rain soon.

The same message sounded through his phone speaker:

"We're sorry, the person you are trying to reach is not available
and does not have their voicemail set up. Please try again later."

Oh, great. He couldn't leave Jemma a message because she didn't have her voicemail set up. He picked up his keys and headed out the door. His pick-up truck was parked outside. He was going to make another truck stop in town.

"Where are you headed?" Beau asked him.

"In town. You need anything?"

"Nope. Jesse's gone down to the supply store to get more fencing supplies."

"Good. I'll be back soon."

"Are you okay?"

"Yeah, why?"

"You look annoyed or something."

He really didn't want to get into anything with his brother right now. He knew Beau would probably ask him about Jemma *again*. Right now, he just couldn't talk about it.

"Just work, that's all. Got to hire a new contractor to paint the old barn."

"Oh, right. Isn't Jesse going to handle that?"

"Yeah, but you know Jesse, he gets caught up in all sorts of projects. Way over his head sometimes."

Luke and Beau smiled.

His brother Jesse always meant well, but sometimes he'd take on more than he could handle and not even ask for help.

But since Luke handled most of the arrangements and oversaw the management of the ranch, he'd sometimes re-assign tasks to other ranch workers.

He started up his truck and made his way off the plot onto the gravel road.

He had no idea why Jemma was trying to reach him, but he had a feeling something was wrong.

Chapter 14

Jemma hoped it wouldn't be too late. She pulled up at the gorgeous *Carsen's Sweet Rivers Ranch*, looking around at the massive land with rolling pastures. It sure was a nice piece of property.

She then glanced at her dead cell phone. The battery had drained to 5% then quickly to zero while she was at the hospital visiting her grandfather. She just started charging her phone again in the car. She'd leave it there until it finished charging.

She got out of the car and closed the door.

She read the sign at the entrance of the retreat:

Chet Carsen's Sweet Rivers Family Ranch and Retreat.
From Our Family to Yours

It made her feel all warm and fuzzy inside for some reason. Genuine love. That was all the vibe she felt whenever she visited there. Especially during the past week when her client, little Jimmy, spent the week there. It had been pure bliss.

"Morning, Ms. Jemma," Beau, Luke's brother said to her as she walked towards Cabin One. She was sure that was the cabin where Luke lived. She didn't see his blue Ford pick-up truck though. Her heart fell.

"Morning, Beau. I was just here to see Luke."

"Oh, sorry, you missed him. He just left."

"Oh?" A wave of disappointment flooded her. Even though his truck wasn't parked outside his cabin, she was hoping somehow he'd be on the land somewhere and that there was a perfectly reasonable explanation why his truck wasn't there. But oh, no. No such luck.

"Is there something I could help you with?" Beau was very welcoming. She noticed that all the brothers were helpful and kind. They each shone a bright smile whenever they spoke to her or anyone.

What a family.

A family she'd love to be part of now. If that were even possible.

"I don't think so. You see..." What was she going to say? She really wanted to tell him the real reason she was there. But there was no way she could do that. Time was running out. She had to ask Luke about getting married in a few days. That seemed almost impossible.

She needed Luke now. She could not wait much longer. Her grandfather was holding out, but he was ill and could go any time now. He didn't have much longer.

Just then Sue Mae came out of the main house.

"I thought that was you," Sue Mae said, a warm smile on her face. "Well, hello stranger."

"Hi Sue Mae. So good to see you again."

"Likewise."

"She's looking for Luke," Beau said.

"Oh, Luke." A sly grin curved Sue Mae's lips. "Yes, of course. Why don't you come to the main house and wait here? He shouldn't be too long. I'll make you some nice sweet tea."

Jemma noticed Beau grinned and shook his head.

"Oh, I don't want to put you out, Sue Mae."

"Oh, nonsense." Sue Mae looked her over. "You look like you could use a nice glass of my special sweet tea. It's good for the soul, you know."

Beau gave his aunt an incredulous look. "Really, Sue Mae?"

"And why not?" Sue Mae said.

Jemma couldn't help but smile.

Later, Jemma sat in the main living room with Sue Mae.

"Mmm, this is so delicious. It's not like any southern sweet tea I've tasted before," Jemma said.

"Thank you. It's my special recipe."

"What else did you put in it?" Jemma observed the nice crystal glass.

"Oh, that's my little secret." Sue Mae grinned. "So you were telling me that Luke asked you to marry him." Sue Mae changed the subject.

"Yes. I'm guessing you had something to do with that." Jemma placed her now empty glass down the table and gave Sue Mae a knowing grin.

"Well, like I said before, I've successfully matched many couples at the church. You know love and marriage is a wonderful thing."

"I know Sue Mae. But that's if you find the right person."

"And Luke is wonderful."

"Oh, I don't doubt that. But..." What was she going to say? That it would only be a marriage on paper only.

"I know what you're thinking," she said, picking up the empty glasses and placing them on the tray to take to the kitchen. "But it *will* work out. Sometimes you just have to leave it to the Lord and put your trust in Him, even if you don't see a way out."

"But I don't even know if it'll work out."

"What's not to work out?"

"We'll have to act like a married couple."

"And what's so bad about that?"

"Never was good at acting."

"Oh, come on now. It's me you're talking to. I've seen you in the church plays, remember?"

"I know. You know what I mean. Memorizing a script is one thing, but faking how I feel?"

"And how do you feel?"

How much should she tell Sue Mae?

Sue Mae was, after all, Luke's adoptive aunt. "I feel as if marriage should be for real. It's a big commitment."

"I know it is. But you never know how it's going to work out."

"Even if we're pretending to be married?"

"I've seen you two together over the week at the retreat. You seemed to go together like a pair of warm mittens."

Jemma really wanted this to work out.

"I don't think he feels the same way. He's been hurt before. Just like me."

"I believe two hurt souls can heal each other with love. Love can heal anything. It's almost like the common thread that pulls everything together." Her tone was soothing.

"I guess you're right. In theory, anyway."

"Oh, come on now. Theory? It can work well in practice too. You just both have to make the best of the situation. You know what they say? That some marriages of conveniences could blossom into marriages of love."

If only.

She wished that would be the case. But Luke seemed bent on never falling in love. He'd told her so himself. Especially after what his ex-wife had done to him. What a terrible thing to have happened to such a nice cowboy like Luke.

Terrible.

She felt sorry for him. He'd given his ex-wife everything. And while he was overseas serving in the military years ago, she'd cheated on him and left him with nothing but a ring and emptiness inside.

Could Jemma even begin to fill that emptiness?

Was she getting in over her head? But she just didn't want a life having an empty marriage that was only real on paper.

She just couldn't do it.

She wished Luke felt the same way that she did.

Why did he blame himself for what his ex-wife did to him though? Luke seemed to think he didn't deserve a second chance at love, but maybe, if he still wanted to get married, they could make this work.

"So how is your dear grandfather?" Sue Mae asked.

"He's...he's pretty much the same. But I've been spending as much time as I can with him."

Jemma didn't want to tell Sue Mae about her grandfather's changed condition just yet.

She had to tell Luke first. It wouldn't be fair to Luke to find out that he was getting married soon through someone else.

A few knitted garments on the couch caught Jemma's attention.

"These are lovely," Jemma said.

"Thank you."

"It's wonderful that you've knitted so many scarves."

Jemma remembered Sue Mae used to knit garments for the drama club. She would knit scarves in wintertime and give one to each member of the drama club. She'd also donated scarves to the troops overseas. And many of her garments she'd give as donations. The scarves were pretty with lovely designs on them. Sometimes she'd have a message sewn on them. Like a scripture or something like that. Talk about creative.

"Thank you, dear. You know scarves are not just warm and cozy but there are health benefits."

"There are?"

"Oh, yes. Wearing a scarf like this can help dilate the blood vessels in the neck muscles and ease tension and it can increase oxygen flow in the muscles. It's one of the most versatile clothing accessories. It dates all the way back from ancient Egypt and in some cultures it marks military rank depending on the style and color."

"Really now?" Jemma hadn't thought about that before. "You know a lot about them."

"Here." She finished knitting the scarf and showed it to Jemma. Jemma read the message on it: *Faith, hope and love.*

Of course.

1 Corinthians 13:4-8.

Jemma's grandfather had given her that scripture to remind her just the other day. And now, she had to keep her faith and hope alive. She had no other choice.

Just then, she heard the door open and close in the foyer. A pair of cowboy boots made a clunking sound on the hardwood floor. There was something authoritative about the sound of cowboy boots on the floor. And in walked a tall, dark, and handsome cowboy.

Luke Carsen.

He had an unreadable expression on his handsome face, though.

Right.

How was she going to tell him they were getting married this week?

Chapter 15

Moments later, after they left the main house and said goodbye to Sue Mae, Luke walked Jemma over to his cabin to talk.

"I was trying to reach you," Luke said.

"I'm sorry, but my phone battery died. I came over because I had to speak to you urgently."

"You do?" He led her inside his cabin.

"It's gorgeous." She looked around, stunned. "I didn't know it would be so breathtaking."

"It's a place to lay my head at night."

"That's an understatement."

She seemed to fit right into his home. It was as if she belonged there.

He then went into the kitchen after giving her a brief tour. "Let me fix you something to eat."

"You cook?"

"Of course I do."

"Oh, no. I didn't mean it like that, I just meant..." She flushed.

"I'm only teasing. What would you like me to make you?"

"Whatever you're having?"

"Well, I can fry some steak and..."

"I'd love that. Here, let me help you."

"Oh, no. You're a guest here."

"It's okay. I want to make myself useful."

He noticed she was awfully kind right now. Not that she wasn't before. But she just seemed so flustered right now, like she wanted desperately to get his approval.

"So what's this urgency?"

"Oh, it's nothing. It's just that...well, I think we're getting married this week."

"What?"

Luke's jaw fell wide open.

"Sorry, Luke. I'm *really* sorry about springing this on you like this. I know I said I'd think about...your proposal, but I just went to see my grandpa yesterday and...well, he's really not doing too well. He doesn't have much time left and well, I...I would really love to make his last wish come true."

Luke didn't know what to say. He was thrilled, of course, that she'd said yes. Well, he took that as a yes to his proposal, but this was happening all so suddenly now. This was going to happen now, wasn't it?

"You sure about this now?" Luke asked.

"Yes. I've never been more sure. My heart feels it's the right thing to do."

"Now, this week's kind of sudden. I hadn't expected to say my vows so soon...but okay, you need it done this week. I'll make it happen."

"You will?" He could feel the excitement rush from her.

"Yes. We'd need to get a marriage licence. I'll make a trip downtown tomorrow."

"Oh, Luke. You have no idea how this makes me feel. I owe you one. Thank you."

Jemma hugged him and he hugged her back.

A wave of delight swept through Luke's body as he held her. Joy bubbled through him. He didn't want to let her go. She felt so right in his arms. What was wrong with him? He wasn't supposed to be falling for her. This would only be a business deal. Nothing more.

He soon pulled away from her, as much as he wanted to keep her in his arms. He had to focus.

"Hey, it's an arrangement," Luke said, softly. "We'll both benefit from this. It will make those we care about happy."

Just saying it out loud made the reality clear as a bell. It was really happening. He was going to be married to this beautiful, lovely woman before him who made his heart sing. Could this really be true? Was he dreaming? He wanted to do this.

"You know it's going to be marriage in name only, right?" he said. "A business arrangement."

He saw her swallow hard. "Y-yes. I know that," she said, her voice soft and low.

"You okay with that?"

"I'll have to be."

"Well, then..." He busied himself getting dinner prepared, seasoning the steaks, and then adding them to the frying pan.

He was on autopilot right now.

He knew the lawyer would be back soon to check up on the boys before handling all the official land transfer papers. At least he could say that he was married. But man, everything was happening so fast.

He took another glance at his beautiful bride to be—in name only, but still. She seemed a little nervous.

Was she going to back out of this deal?

Chapter 16

Later, Luke and Jemma sat down to dinner at his round oak dinner table. She could visualize a family having dinner there.

The dining room was cozy and warm. Luke had a few Christmas decorations up and a small tree in the corner by the fireplace. It was certainly more than what she had up in the house. Since Grandpa had been in the hospital long term care unit, she hadn't bothered to get all festive in the home. No wonder the Christmas spirit was missing from her own house.

But she felt the spirit of the season there with Luke tonight.

She felt all kinds of wonderful things. Especially when they embraced earlier, after he'd agreed to marry her.

Oh, those sweet emotions that washed over her like the waves of the ocean, were a delight to her soul. She felt tingles swirl through her belly and all over her body. She wished he hadn't pulled away so soon, she wanted to be in his embrace forever. The sweet scent of his cologne and those strong arms made her feel so at home.

She could not believe he didn't back off when she told him they could be getting married this week.

He'd given it some thought and just said he'd "make it happen."

Make it happen.

What a guy.

Talk about a positive, take charge kind of guy.

She then thought about her own *Grant-A-Wish* foundation and how she told her clients whatever their wishes, she'd make it happen for them.

Well, it was thrilling to have that sentiment given to her in return. She'd never met anyone like that before who could move worlds around for her to make things happen.

She'd never met anyone like Luke Carsen before. Lovely on the outside and lovely on the inside.

Jemma carefully cut a piece of steak off and stuck the fork in it to lift it to her lips. She took a bite and wow! She couldn't believe the juicy taste of the steak.

Her husband-to-be could really cook!

"*Mmm*, delicious. It's so juicy."

"Thanks. It's nothing."

"Oh, no. It's *something*," she said.

The steak wasn't the only delicious item at the table though. Luke was gorgeous. Stunning. She couldn't believe this was really happening.

This week, they would be husband and wife. She would be Mrs. Jemma Carsen. The thought made her tingle inside with delight.

She felt giddy with excitement and a mixture of nervousness. Could she really pull this off?

After dinner, they sat in his living room and talked about the arrangements. Luke had called the pastor after dinner and they had a good long talk on the phone.

"So I'll head down to city hall in the morning and get all the documents we need."

"Okay. And I'll get a dress and everything. I'll need to contact the hospital to let them know what time."

"The hospital?"

"Oh, yes. You see, Grandpa's too weak to leave. They said we can have the ceremony there. Is that okay?"

He looked puzzled for a moment then nodded. "Sure. No problem. We'll do it then."

A warm feeling slid inside of her. Luke was amazing in every way—and so accommodating. She couldn't even imagine who would want to hurt such a nice and noble cowboy like Luke.

"I really want to thank you again," Jemma said.

"Hey, we both need to do this, remember?"

"I know, but I appreciate your devotion to making it happen in this special way. It really means a lot to my grandfather....and to me."

She thought she saw a hint of color in his cheeks, but that was probably from the glow of the fireplace.

"Well, I guess, I'll give you a proper tour of the place now since I didn't get to show you where everything is earlier," he said, getting up.

She got up and noticed his collection of books in the bookshelf. She walked over to the shelf and saw a row of her favorite novels.

"You read C. C. Dale too?"

He looked surprised. "You're a fan?"

"Of course. Who isn't? I love her romance novels. They're so sweet and full of wisdom and hope. I can't get enough of them. It's a shame she stopped writing though. There isn't much information about her online."

"Well, some writers like to remain private or anonymous."

"Well, it's wonderful what she's done. Giving readers hope and love through the pages."

He smiled and his gaze met hers.

For a moment, they stood there. Then...

He turned his gaze from her. "Come, I'll show you to your room," he said.

"My room?"

"Yes, we'll be sleeping in separate rooms after we tie the knot, of course."

"Right." She swallowed hard. "Of course."

Since her lease was almost up at the house, the timing couldn't be more perfect. Sue Mae was right about keeping the faith that things would work out.

But this would not be a real marriage. She'd soon need to find another place to stay and figure out her finances and apply for some freelance work.

Marriage in name only.

She tried to hide her disappointment, but that was the arrangement, wasn't it? It was a marriage-in-name-only deal.

Still, a part of her, a very big part of her, wanted that deal to be real. She loved being in Luke's presence. She felt so protected, so loved.

The way he was determined to make her dreams come true touched her heart in so many ways. He was like her knight in shining armor.

Only, she could tell his armor was not there just to protect his body, but his heart too. It looked as if she would not be able to penetrate that armour any time soon. He was determined to keep her at a distance. She just felt it.

But that was the arrangement, right? In name only. It didn't look as if he'd be changing his mind any time soon.

But then how could they have so much in common? They loved to watch the sunset together, to dream, to help others, to read the same romance novels.

"You never pegged me as a guy who reads romance novels."

"It's like you said, there's nothing wrong with love and hope, is there?"

"Nope. There isn't."

***

"Okay, come again now?" Mandy said over the phone that evening after Jemma returned to her house.

"I'm getting married this week."

"Girl, are you for real?"

"I sure hope so. Either that or I'm in some kind of dream."

They both giggled over the phone.

"I'm so happy for you, surprised, but happy."

"I know it's sudden, but Grandpa's not doing so well and well..." She didn't want to tell Mandy too much right now. After all, she didn't want to get into Luke's business. They'd both made an arrangement, but it wasn't safe to tell the whole world it would be a fake marriage of convenience. And she certainly didn't want her grandfather to get wind of that either.

He'd be broken-hearted if he thought she'd done this just to please him and that she'd be getting divorced soon.

Then another thought struck her.

How long would they remain married? She would love to have children one day. How was that going to happen if their marriage was fake—in name only?

"So you're going to need something borrowed, right?" Mandy interrupted her thoughts.

"Yes, I guess I will."

"Well, you can borrow my pearl necklace. My grandmother gave it to me."

"Oh, Mandy. Are you sure?"

"Course, I'm sure. You're my bestie."

"Thank you so much. It really means a lot."

"Hey, I'm just so happy for you."

"Now, what about your wedding dress?"

"I'm going to keep it traditional—nothing too over-the-top."

This had to look real. It had to have an air of authenticity about it. It had to be magical. No one was supposed to know it was a marriage of convenience outside of the family. She still wanted to have a beautiful dress. They would be taking pictures, after all. And it might be the only time she even *got* married.

She'd always dreamt of walking down the aisle in a "fairy tale" ballgown, with a fitted bodice, flairs at the waist, and a full skirt. That style was ideal for most body types and looked great on curvy thighs like hers, since it hid the lower body.

She knew that was not going to happen on such short notice. She'd have to improvise. But she couldn't go to the hospital bedside of her grandfather to get married in jeans.

What was she going to do about a wedding dress on such short notice?

Chapter 17

This was really happening, wasn't it? Luke thought to himself two days later.

Luke managed to secure the marriage license a couple days ago. He also re-assigned his morning ranch duties to his brothers, Blake and Carter, so that he could prepare and get fitted into a suit for his wedding day.

He gathered his other brothers, Beau, his best man, Jesse, Chase, and Zack for the ceremony at the Sweet Rivers Hospital long term care wing.

It was early afternoon and they made their way to the *Hope Chapel.* The long-term care division of the hospital was an immaculate, residence-style building with medical facilities.

Jemma had once told him that she wanted the best for her grandfather. She gave up her apartment and used her savings to get him into the best facility and she was glad she did.

Luke had to admit that Jemma was all heart.

The guests were already there waiting for them in the little hospital chapel.

It was a small gathering. Sue Mae was there. And so was Sister Ellie and his brothers.

He was glad Pastor Dave from the Sweet Rivers Church was able to squeeze this surprise wedding into his schedule. He was sure Sue Mae had a bit of persuading there.

Festive garlands decorated the entrance of the doorway. Lights were everywhere. There was a beautiful glowing Christmas tree with flickering lights in the lobby in front of the chapel. It provided an enchanted atmosphere. But seeing his bride-to-be, Jemma, blew his mind.

As she walked down the aisle in a flowing white dress, her grandfather on the stretcher, being wheeled down the aisle beside her with the help of a nurse, brought tears of joy to his eyes as his eyes misted over.

He admired Jemma deeply. The way she wanted to make others happy. The woman was all heart and soul. He'd do anything for her. Anything. She just had that way about her.

Moments later, the ceremony began.

"Do you, Luke Carsen promise to be a loving friend and partner in marriage, to talk and to listen, to trust and appreciate, to respect and cherish Jemma? Do you promise to support, comfort, and strengthen her through life's joys and sorrows? Do you promise to share hopes and dreams as you both build your lives together? Will you strive to build a home that is full of respect and honor, filled with peace, happiness, and love? Do you promise to always be open and honest with Jemma, and cherish her for as long as you both shall live?"

He breathed deeply, his heart beating hard and fast in his chest. "I do," he said proudly, looking deep into Jemma's pretty brown eyes.

He swallowed hard. He could not believe this was a marriage in name only. Something seemed so wrong about that. But then he glanced at his family. He knew what this meant for them and his adoptive father's last wish. Still, Jemma took his breath away.

Why on earth was he feeling this way if this was supposed to only be a business arrangement?

It was Jemma's turn now.

"Do you, Jemma promise to be a loving friend and partner in marriage, to talk and to listen, to trust and appreciate, to respect and cherish Luke? Do you promise to support, comfort, and strengthen him through life's joys and sorrows? Do you promise to share hopes and dreams as you both build your lives together? Will you strive to build a home that is full of respect and honor, filled with peace, happiness, and love? Do you promise to always be open and honest with Luke, and cherish him for as long as you both shall live?"

He noticed Jemma took a deep breath, too.

Was she just as nervous as he was?

Funny thing, he never thought he'd be this nervous given the circumstances, but he felt it all right.

She paused for a moment and his stomach fell. Was she changing her mind? Was she going to call it off?

"I do." Her words finally slid out through her beautiful shapely lips as she captured his gaze with hers and excitement rushed over him.

"Jemma and Luke, you have expressed your love to one another through the commitment and promises you have just made. It is with these in mind that I pronounce you husband and wife."

Luke's grin was wider than the ocean right now. He could see his brother Beau nodding him on in a loving brotherly way from the corner of his eye.

"You have kissed each other before," Pastor Dave continued. If only the pastor knew the truth. Luke hadn't touched Jemma's lips yet. Though he'd wanted to many times ever since he met her.

"But today the feeling will be new," Pastor Dave continued. "You will no longer be friends but husband and wife and can now seal the agreement with a kiss. Today, your kiss will be a promise." Luke breathed hard. He'd never been so nervous before. It was only a kiss, right?

"You may now kiss the bride," the pastor said.

And with those words, Luke gazed deeply into his new bride Jemma's beautiful soft brown eyes and lifted the veil, every breath he took was filled with butterflies in his stomach. She looked hopefully into his eyes as he lowered his head down to hers and pressed his lips to her soft lips and kissed her.

Their kiss was slow and beautiful, deep, and magical.

He'd felt warmth explode in his belly like never before.

Man, this was just a kiss, but it was so much more. His whole body felt alive with euphoria. He felt as if he were in some enchanted place.

She kissed him with the same deep passion.

How could this not be real?

This was supposed to be a fake, quick kiss, but it was turning into something more. Something he didn't know if he could carry through.

He broke off softly. She looked stunned at first.

Cheers and congratulations erupted from the guests.

They were now husband and wife.

But she looked disappointed that he'd cut the kiss short.

He loved that kiss, but it frightened him with what it really meant. He'd agreed to get married again. That was the deal. But falling in love was not an option.

Chapter 18

That kiss.

Oh, my goodness, that kiss.

Jemma's heart was filled with love and hope and a whole bucket full of crazy emotions later that evening. The memory of that sweet, passionate kiss with her husband rocked her world. She'd never been kissed like *that* before.

Where did he learn to kiss like that?

She wanted to ask him that as they danced in the festively decorated party room at the care facility.

Her grandfather was elated as he laid in the stretcher watching on, his nurse at his side. She was ever so thankful they were able to make this happen for him.

God bless him. God bless them all.

"You look *beautiful*, Jemma," Luke said as they danced and he looked lovingly into her eyes.

This is real. This had to be real. He could not be faking this.

"Thank you. So do you. I mean, you look gorgeous today in your tux and your cowboy hat."

"Thank you for doing this, Jemma."

"Thank *you*, Luke and on such short notice," she whispered to him as they danced to the music playing over the speakers.

Luke and his family had arranged catering for the wedding party and included all the staff and other residents. She hadn't realized before just how well off the family was. Money certainly was no object for them. Not that it mattered to Jemma at all. But she was grateful they were able to take over and help out with expenses.

A sinking feeling slid into her tummy. Why couldn't this be for real?

Her friend Mandy took the afternoon off work to be her maid of honor and Luke's brother Beau was his best man.

The family looked so overcome with joy. But right now, Jemma should be the happiest woman alive, married to a gorgeous cowboy. A man of honor, love, and charm. Instead she had the dreaded feeling that after tonight it would be all business and nothing more.

Then again, the way he was with her tonight made her feel there was no way he could be faking it.

Maybe once they returned to his cabin at the ranch he'd change his mind and tell her they were going to live like husband and wife in every sense of the word.

Would that be too much to ask? But then again, it wasn't part of the deal, was it?

"I'm so happy, you have no idea," Grandpa said to Jemma and Luke later. "Luke, you and Jemma make me very proud. I can see how much in love you both are with each other."

Jemma's throat tightened with emotion. She was going to burst into tears any moment now. How could this be? She was thrilled her grandfather was so happy, but Luke and she had gotten married to make him happy—and to fulfill Luke's adoptive father's will stipulation.

After the dance, they'd both went over to the side to sit beside Grandpa Smith and the nurse. The nurse had gotten up to give them privacy. Grandpa held both her hand and Luke's as each of them got to his side. Luke on one side of her grandpa and Jemma on the other side.

Then Beau took out his camera. "Smile. Say *Christmas*."

They all grinned and said "Christmas" together.

"Let me see that," Grandpa said, weakly. Beau showed him the camera's digital display. Grandpa's eyes filled with joy.

"I never thought I'd live to see the day. You've both made me so happy, because I know that you'll be happy together after I leave. This is what love is about. Family. And Jemma and Luke, you're going to have beautiful children together."

Jemma was going to cry now. This should be the happiest day of her life. So why did she feel as if something was missing?

She changed her mind. She didn't want to go through with this. She was not going to stay in a marriage of convenience. She wanted the real deal. And she felt in her heart that Luke wanted it too.

But what if she was wrong?

Chapter 19

Later that night, Luke took his new bride, Jemma, to Cabin One on the ranch.

"Well, this is *our* place now." He picked her up and carried her over the threshold, as was tradition, while the others looked on from their cabins.

A sign posted on the door read "Just Married!"

He'd done it.

This was the deal, wasn't it? He knew he felt something but he knew he'd have to push those feelings aside.

Love wasn't part of the deal.

After the door closed behind them, he knew he had to close off the feelings he had earlier at the wedding, but man, it was hard to do. He was really falling for Jemma but that was dangerous territory.

"I can't believe we're married," Jemma said.

"Me either. But we did it."

"I know." She stood there in front of him, looking up into his eyes.

Was she expecting him to kiss her again? Lord only knew how much he wanted to, but that would complicate matters.

"Jemma, I think we should keep this strictly business." He could see the disappointment on her face as he said those words.

Oh, no. This was not how he wanted the night to end.

"I know." Her tone was very matter-of-fact, but he could sense the hurt behind it.

"No, I don't think you know. I'm a damaged man, Jemma. I can't fall in love again."

"Of course you can," she said, hopefully.

She really wanted this, didn't she?

Maybe he should have made this clear as a condition.

"No, I can't," he said, turning from her. He made his way into the kitchen. "Can I get you a drink?"

"No, you can get me your love."

"What?"

"Luke, I know you feel the same way I feel about you."

"Hey, we've only known each other a short while."

"When it comes to true love, it doesn't have to take that long. Some people can know each other a whole lifetime and not connect. But *we* connect. One thing about my grandfather is that he's always spot on with people. He could tell we feel something for each other too."

"I love your grandpa, *our* grandpa now. But Jemma, let's not do this. I can't bear for this to get complicated."

"What's so complicated about it? We feel something. I felt it in our kiss, Luke. Don't tell me that wasn't real."

He wished he could say that, but the truth was, it *was* real to him. He felt something, but he had to let it go.

"I'll show you to your room, Jemma."

"Luke, I don't want us to live like this. We're married."

"Whoa there, we had an agreement, Jemma. In name only."

"And agreements can be amended." She arched her brow, hopefully.

"Nope. Not this time."

"What?" Her voice was soft and filled with surprise.

"I'll take you to your room. We'll talk about it in the morning."

"I'll find my way to the room, thank you." Her tone was firm this time.

Oh, no.

Did he just upset his new bride?

Chapter 20

The following week, Luke and Jemma went to the church to help wrap some presents for needy children in the community as part of the traditional Christmas gift-a-thon.

"Well, look at the happy couple," Pastor Dave said as they walked into the basement of the church where the wrapping took place.

"Hello Pastor," Jemma said brightly.

"Pastor," Luke said, tilting his cowboy hat.

"You two really are good together," the pastor commented. "I'm so happy for you, that you both found each other."

"Thank you."

"No other couple has wrapped so many presents in such a short span of time. How did you do it?" Pastor Dave asked later that afternoon.

"It's teamwork," Jemma said.

"That's what love does, doesn't it?" Pastor Dave said.

Luke said nothing for a moment.

Jemma wondered what Luke was feeling.

If only the pastor knew. They were both sleeping in separate rooms. No one could tell, that was the problem. They were so *good* together. Why couldn't Luke see that?

Later, they went back to the ranch and Jemma said she always wanted to take a sleigh ride. So Luke got her up on a sleigh and they rode on the ranch for a while.

She tried to snuggle up to him in the sleigh but then...he distanced himself—again.

"Luke why do you keep doing that?"

"Doing what?"

"Keeping your distance like that."

"I already told you, Jemma."

"Yes, you're fighting those feelings inside of you. I'm not your ex, Luke."

His body stiffened. "I didn't say you were."

"But you're treating me this way. You refuse to watch the sunsets with me anymore, we have so much fun doing all these Christmas activities and yet when we start to get close, you pull away."

"Listen, Jemma, it's better that way."

"For whom? For you or for me?"

"Jemma, this is over." He stopped the sleigh ride and got off, then helped her off.

"What's over?"

"The ride and the discussion."

With those words, Luke left, leaving Jemma feeling too stunned to speak.

One week later...

It had been two weeks since she said her vows to Luke Carsen and things still hadn't changed.

Well, she knew they'd changed inside for her *and* Luke but he just wouldn't admit it.

"Is everything all right between you two?" Sue Mae said to Jemma when Jemma walked over to the main house to help bake gingerbread cookies.

It was a week before Christmas and Grandpa was still holding on at the Sweet Rivers Hospital Long-Term Care facility.

Jemma was so grateful. They were baking gingerbread cookies for the staff and residents there. Last week, they baked for the children's homes in the area.

It was a delight to see the joy on the children's faces and to spend time with Luke's family on the ranch. It was so festive and warm around there.

"Could be better," Jemma said.

She didn't want to say too much to Sue Mae, but she knew Sue Mae was perceptive. Sue Mae was now, after all, her aunt-in-law, right?

"Luke and I want two different things."

"Two different things?"

"Yes, I want a real marriage and he...he just doesn't want to see how good we are together. My feelings can't be wrong. I can sense his emotions."

Just then, Jemma felt a vibration from her pocket. She stopped what she was doing and slid out her cell phone.

It was a call from the hospital.

Her heart stopped.

Chapter 21

"You know I don't believe in all this marriage business, but man, you two are really good together," Beau said to Luke as he finished feeding the horses.

"It's in name only."

"Have you thought about what Sue Mae said? You seem to brush Jemma off whenever she wants to get close to you. She wanted to help you out on the ranch and instead you told her to buddy up with one of us."

"It's for the best."

"For whom, Luke? We all want to see you happy, man."

Just then Jesse approached them, a worried look on his face.

"Jesse, you all right?"

"I'm good, but it's Jemma."

Luke's heart jumped hard in his chest.

"Is she okay?" Luke asked, concerned. His breath quickened, the thought of anything happening to Jemma made him go crazy inside.

"No. Well, she's gone."

"What? Gone? What do you mean she's gone?"

"She left an hour ago, man. Her...I think her grandpa passed."

Luke's heart squeezed hard in his chest. Guilt tore through him. Memories of his own adoptive father's death came flooding back to hit him hard.

But what hit him harder was the way Jemma had tried to get so close to him all these weeks and he'd kept pushing her away. Now, her only blood relative was gone, and she was alone.

The last thing he wanted was for her to be alone or to feel alone.

He wasn't a good husband, not even a good *fake* husband. He should have been there by her side.

"I'm heading there now," Luke said.

Moments later, he got into his pick-up truck and drove out to Sweet Rivers Hospital.

He'd tried calling Jemma, but she didn't pick up her phone. He imagined she would be too overcome with grief right now.

He only hoped it wouldn't be too late to reach out to her.

***

Later, when he arrived at the hospital, he went inside and the staff told him Jemma was in the chapel. He made his way over there and he tapped lightly on the door and opened it.

Jemma was there knelt down at the altar, the same altar where they'd exchanged vows that day a few weeks ago.

His heart tugged inside.

He instinctively went over there and knelt down beside her, pulling her into his arms.

Chapter 22

Luke surprised Jemma when he'd arrived. She didn't even bother to call him when she got the news that her ninety-year-old grandfather had gone to be with the Lord.

She just made her way to the Sweet Rivers Hospital on her own, feeling she was all alone now in the world. Married to a man who insisted it wasn't a real marriage, despite the feelings she was getting from him.

But now...

His warm hands on her shoulders helped her through this. That sense of comfort. Protection. The sweet scent of his cologne wafted to her nose. She felt his energies. She really felt it more than she'd felt it before.

She turned around to face him.

"Jemma, I'm so sorry about your grandpa."

"Thank you." Her voice was weak and soft.

"I'm here for you, Jemma. I want you to know that."

"Are you?" she asked softly. "I'm sorry, I shouldn't have said that."

"No, you have every right to say that."

"They told me he was very happy and peaceful. They said that he was laughing and making jokes and saying how he was thrilled that he got to see us married. He'd said now he was *ready*. Ready to go to be with his wife, my late grandmother."

"He lived a good long life, didn't he?" Luke said, gently.

"Yes, he did. I only wished..."

"Wished what?" Luke's voice was soft and reassuring.

"Nothing."

"No, what is it?"

"My grandfather said, because he knew we were happily married, he felt at peace. But...but..."

"We are," Luke finished her sentence to her surprise, but the ending was not what she expected from him.

"What do you mean?"

"Jemma, I've thought about it for a while now and especially now on the way over here. Life's too short to not give all you can, to not love and appreciate the one you're with. I love you, Jemma. I have from the moment I first laid eyes on you, if that's possible. I never believed in love at first sight and it terrified me, but then when my brother said you'd left... I thought he meant you'd left me, and I just couldn't handle that. All of a sudden, I couldn't see the rest of my life without you in it."

"What are you saying, Luke?"

"After we leave here, from this chapel, I want us to be a real couple. I want to give it a chance, if you'll let me. We're family now, Jemma. You'll always have me."

"Oh, Luke, of course, I will. You'll always have me too."

Epilogue

This Christmas Day was the most special Christmas Jemma could ever remember. She had a family again. A real family.

The Carsens all gathered around the large festively decorated Christmas tree in the living room and made wishes and opened up presents by the fireplace.

Everyone was present at the main house, Sue Mae, Sister Ellie, Luke, Beau, Jesse, Chase, Jake, Zack, and Billy the cook who was like family. Cocoa the dog was also with them.

"Your father, Chet, would have been so proud to see us all here on this anniversary giving thanks and spending time together as a family," Sue Mae said. "And Jemma, welcome to the family." A warm smile spread across Sue Mae's face.

Jemma's heart squeezed with joy. "Thank you. I'm so proud to be a Carsen," she looked lovingly into Luke's eyes and this time he did not look the other way, he returned the gaze as he hugged her close to him.

She would forever cherish this time and she could feel her grandfather's spirit around her, knowing he is looking down on them and feeling the love, seeing them happy.

***

Jemma could see Beau sitting to the side, gazing out the window, watching the snow fall. She really hoped he would be as happy as his brother Luke. She'd learned that his wife had died in a crash after they had an argument. But she was with someone else. That could not have been easy for him.

"And Beau," Sue Mae said. "I hope to see you settle down soon."

"Oh, no. Not me." Beau was adamant.

"Look at how happy Luke and Jemma are."

"I know, Sue Mae, and we're all happy for them. I don't think it's going to work that way for me."

"Never say never, Beau. Love can make things happen."

"And a little matchmaking on the side, won't hurt either," Luke said, with a smile.

Jemma felt the love and the positive energy with the family on this special Christmas Day.

Yes, it's true, *"Three things will last forever—faith, hope, and love—and the greatest of these is love."*

***

Thank you for reading *Her Christmas Cowboy*. Those Carsen brothers are really something, aren't they? Will Beau find true love again? Read book two in the Carsen Brothers of Sweet Rivers Ranch *Her Cowboy Hero*, available now!

Here's a sneak peek...

Her Cowboy Hero

Beau Carsen wants to put the past behind him after his wife left him then sadly died in a tragic accident, but he finds himself in a hot spot. He needs a new wife to honor his late adoptive father's will in order to stay on the family ranch...can he go down that marriage road again?

Lucky Laneson rescues pets, but right now she's the one who needs to be rescued when she finds herself out of a job, and homeless thanks to her unscrupulous landlord. She needs a place to stay, but when she learns Beau Carsen needs a convenient wife, she wonders if she could occupy a place in Beau's heart?

Chapter 1

Beau Carsen finished applying a coat of paint to the barn door. He took off his cowboy hat, smoothed his hair, and replaced his hat. The warm spring weather and the soothing wind relaxed him.

This was good living. On *Chet Carsen's Sweet Rivers Family Ranch and Retreat*, the ranch founded by his late adopted father, one of the oldest working cowboys in Texas at the time. Chet Carsen, who passed away last year at age eighty, was also the secret pen name C. C. Dale, under which he co-wrote Christian love stories with his wife. Love was what got him through the difficulties of the war, beautiful poems, and scriptures his wife would send to him while he was away serving in the military, to heal his spirit and give him the courage he needed. That's why it was so important to Chet to share that love with his family and all who knew him. Due to his injuries sustained from the war Chet couldn't have children of his own, but that hadn't stopped him and his wife in their later years from adopting kids from the foster care system. Chet always believed in counting his blessings not his troubles and he instilled that in his adopted children. Chet always said God had a special purpose for him and that was to help kids in need after the war.

Beau Carsen was one of them. And he was forever grateful after coming from a broken home. That's why, after Chet passed, he wanted to honor his last wishes, even though it seemed impossible.

The ranch was a haven for Beau. He loved fixing things, helping his other brothers take care of the livestock and occasional guests that came to the retreat. The ranch was one of the largest in Sweet Rivers, Texas, and had over a dozen log cabins in addition to the main house and lodge. Each brother lived in their own cabin and were practically neighbors. They'd visit each other often and raid one another's fridge, if they weren't at the main house.

His aunt Sue Mae, who was Chet's twin sister, took over the main house after Chet and his wife passed and insisted the boys come over for dinner at least once a week in the main house, even though each log cabin was equipped with its own facilities and room for a family.

And speaking of family.

"Beau," Sue Mae, Beau's aunt, and the unofficial family and church matchmaker, dropped by, wearing her cowboy boots and jeans and a knitted shawl.

"Yes, Sue Mae?"

Sue Mae insisted on being called just that, she never liked anyone calling her auntie for some reason.

"How're you doing?"

"Good." He kept it short and sweet, but he knew what was coming next.

It had been a few months now since his brother, Luke, broke the sacred pact to never remarry. Especially since the boys had been through a rough time in their previous relationships. They each had their own shares of heartbreak.

After Chet adopted them from the foster care system, they grew up on the ranch, a safe place. It gave them all a head start in life. Later, some of his brothers followed in his footsteps and served in the military. After 9/11, they'd felt that call to duty to serve and protect. After their tour of duties, they each branched off into other work. They moved off the ranch into the city, up north, and all over the country. But when Chet's age affected his work on the ranch and he got ill, the men all moved back to help save and keep the family ranch.

But it was late last year when Chet's hand-written will was found—his most recent will.

Joe, the family lawyer had the reading and stated that in order to remain on the family ranch, they had to be a family, and since Chet knew they tried to make it work in the past, he encouraged them to never give up on love. Part of the condition of staying on the ranch and keeping it included filling the cabins with a wife and family of their own.

It was after all the ranch's motto: *From our family to yours.* How could they not honor Chet's last wishes in his will?

Luke was insistent, after his ex-wife betrayed him, to never marry again, but he ended up getting married for the sake of the will, and then he fell in love with his convenient bride. But Beau was going to keep that promise to never fall in love again.

Still, his brother Luke lucked out with a sweet girl, Jemma, who owned her own *Grant-A-Wish app*, a foundation that helped ill people make their wishes come true.

"You know you'll have to fulfill your dear father's last wishes, right?" Sue Mae continued.

"Yes, Sue Mae, but like I said, I'm not a marrying man. Not anymore."

"Oh, come on now, Beau. Don't do that to yourself."

"Sue Mae!"

"Beau!"

He sighed and observed the texture of the red paint on the barn. It was smooth and silky. The new coat really made a difference.

"That's going to take a lot of work and time. You sure you don't need help?" Sue Mae asked with her brow raised.

He knew what she was getting at.

"Nope. Got plenty of time. Not for a woman."

"Beau, I'm really sorry about what happened with your...your late wife."

His heart squeezed in his chest. The pain was too great to even think about. He said nothing for a moment.

"But you need to move forward, Beau."

"She was going to leave me." He finally said it out loud. "You know she was with another man in that accident?"

"I know, darling. I know."

"I probably pushed her away."

"No you didn't, Beau. Stop blaming yourself."

"I can't get close to people, Sue Mae. You know that. *She* knew that. That's why she was off with some other guy and then...then that accident happened."

They'd crashed the car; her boyfriend was at the wheel when it happened. The news tore him apart in so many ways.

He'd left New York after that horrific tragedy and came back to the ranch at that time to help his elderly adoptive father manage things. He'd only intended to help his brothers out then head back to New York, but then his heart fell in love with ranch over again. And that was where he wanted to stay.

"Painting barn doors and mending fences is one thing, Sue Mae. Mending the heart is another."

Sue Mae stood silent for a moment, the wind rustling through her silver-streaked dark hair.

"Oh, Beau. You've really been hurt. You know love can heal all wounds. The Lord intended for people to love and to be with one another. You just need to find the right woman who can open up your heart. I think I may have someone for you. You know I know everybody at the church."

He grinned to himself in spite of the situation. What Sue Mae meant was that she knew everybody's *business* at the church. She was the loveable chatty program director. A human news bulletin and active in the women's ministry.

She knew who was looking for love and who wasn't. Bless her soul.

"No, Sue Mae. I appreciate what you're trying to do. And I'm glad it worked out for Luke. This is one son that won't be able to honor that condition in Chet's will."

Chapter 2

Lucky Laneson didn't feel so lucky right now. In fact, it was ironic that her folks named her Lucky. Her life hadn't exactly been easy street. And that street was about to be closed with a detour sign.

"Sorry, Lucky," her boss Steve Daniels said to her. "You've been so amazing with the animals at the rescue mission."

"Hey, it's not your fault," she said.

"I know, but I wished things had been different. You're all heart."

"I'm just glad I can take little Biscuit home and give her a safe place to stay." She cuddled the orange tabby to her chest.

Lucky knew they were going to put Biscuit to sleep if she wasn't adopted by the end of the day yesterday. She just couldn't let that happen. No way.

She'd always wanted another furry feline since her last one had passed a few years ago. It had been hard to get over that loss. But now, she would have Biscuit.

The Sweet Rivers Rescue Shelter was a popular animal refugee facility but had to shut its doors due to lack of revenue.

Her heart sank just thinking about it.

Such a wonderful cause. Luckily, they were able to safely place many of the animals before closing its doors. Today was Lucky's last day at the shelter. She also had her own blog *Lucky Laneson's Tips* including her *Adopt, Don't Shop* weekly segment, as part of a national campaign to raise awareness about the wonderful benefits of adopting rescue pets instead of purchasing puppies from pet stores.

Though she'd been getting tons of traffic to her blog and a lot of affiliate marketing income to help pay her bills and help take care of her younger sister, losing her job at the rescue mission would blow her budget and put a huge strain on her finances, to put it lightly.

There was no way she could depend on her income from her blog. It was way too unstable, to say the least.

What was she going to do now?

"Biscuit is lucky to have you, Lucky," Steve said with a grin. He was a nice older gentleman in his late sixties and took over the mission from his father, but sadly, the accountant had not managed things in the best way. Steve had been so focused, like Lucky, on helping the pets, but not on the sustainability of the business model and finances of the facility. He was already in over his head in debt. Much like Lucky.

She was adopted too, and knew what it was like to not have a home for a while as she'd been in the foster care system before her adoption. Maybe, that's why she gravitated towards helping others and especially those without a home, like the loveable pets that came to the shelter, some of them from traumatic situations. She and the staff nurtured them and cared for them and worked hard to get them placed in the loving homes they deserved.

Now, it looked as if Lucky would need a bit of good luck too.

"If you ever need a reference, just let me know," Steve said.

She'd need a whole lot more than just a reference. She'd need a place to stay and a new job. Where was she going to find that? Not to mention a place that was pet-friendly with little Biscuit, her newest family member.

"Thanks, Steve. And likewise, if you need a good word for anything, let me know."

She could see the emotion in his eyes. They were like a family team there. But she guessed all things came to an end eventually.

Why did this feel like another rejection though?

Just when she thought her luck had changed and things were finally picking up in her life, this had to go and happen. Out of the blue.

Yep, she'd only just found out about the finances, or lack of finances, for the pet rescue mission in the past month. She'd been working there for two and a half years now. She really thought she had a future with them.

"Well, just let me know if you need anything," Steve added.

It was an awkward goodbye.

Lucky had no idea what she was going to do next.

She left the center with Biscuit in her arms and made her way to the parking lot. She reached for her keys and pulled them out. The starter wouldn't work so she manually got into and started her old car, Bessie. She named many of the things close to her. And why not? They were her only friends. Well, sort of. She had a few nice church friends at the Sweet Rivers Church. Especially Sue Mae, the program director. She'd been a friend and a great listening ear. It was so easy to talk to Sue Mae. She was like the mother Lucky never had.

Her adoptive parents were an older retired couple when they adopted her and her sister. Sadly, they passed away recently. So, it was just she and her sister, Josie now.

Just then a call came into her cell phone. Thankfully, she hadn't pulled out of the parking lot yet. She picked it up. It was her sister.

"Josie, are you all right?" Lucky asked.

"No. Lucky, you need to come quick."

"What's wrong?"

There was silence on the other end.

"Josie, what's wrong? Are you okay?"

Her heart stopped beating for a moment.

"No. He's back. You need to come quick."

Her Cowboy Hero (Available now!)

***

For more information on sweet romances that fill your heart with joy, or to sign up for updates on new releases, you can send a message to Marie Richards at pageturningstories@gmail.com She loves to hear from readers.